I tapped lightly on
still refused to look

Finally, I opened the
sideways, hanging ou
open and staring at me. And one of those stupid chopsticks was stuck beneath her ribcage. I heard someone screaming, but it took several seconds before I realized it was me.

Other mysteries by Nancy Mehl

In the Dead of Winter
Bye Bye Bertie

For Whom the Wedding Bell Tolls

An Ivy Towers Mystery

Nancy Mehl

Dedication:

Grandmothers are one of God's special blessings. My friend, Shauna Sparlin, remembers her grandmother, Bula Tuell, as someone who helped to instill character in those around her. She lived her faith every day. My own grandmother, Kathleen Holderby, was the same way. She loved God and taught me to do the same. This book is dedicated to Bula and Kathleen. They were instrumental in creating the fictional character of Bitty Flanagan as well as shaping the real-life lives of those who loved them. Through Bitty, Shauna and I share our wonderful grandmothers with all of you.

Acknowledgments:

As always, my thanks to Deputy Sheriff Robert P. (Pat) Taylor from Kingman County, Kansas. Your help has been crucial! Thank you to my "Mandarin specialists," Ken Chau and Kevin Hill. And to my husband, Norman, and my son, Danny: Thank you for all your love and support.

ISBN 978-1-60260-132-1

Cover design: Kirk DouPonce, DogEared Design
Cover Illustration: Jody Williams

Our mission is to publish and distribute inspirational products offering exceptional value and biblical encouragement to the masses.

Printed in the U.S.A.

Planning a wedding is a lot like planning a funeral. There's a church and a minister. People dress up and food is served. If you are the star of the event, what you wear is very important. Your makeup is crucial and shouldn't be overdone; otherwise guests will look at you and say, "She just doesn't look natural." The biggest *difference* between the two ceremonies is that you get more rest during the funeral. However, you may actually wish for death by the time the wedding is over.

I expressed these feelings to my best friend, Emily Taylor, over lunch at a coffee shop in Hugoton. We'd just left the bridal shop where I'd tried on every dress they had and found absolutely nothing. Don't get me wrong, their dresses were beautiful. They just weren't *me.*

"We can drive to Dodge City," Emily said helpfully. "Maybe you'll find your dress there."

I shook my head. "I doubt it. For some reason, nothing I've seen *feels* right. Maybe I'm just not the wedding dress type."

Emily reached over to touch my arm, her long chestnut hair falling over her slim shoulder. "Ivy, you're getting married. That *makes* you the 'wedding dress type.'" She smiled sweetly, which was easy for her since she is the epitome of sweetness. I felt like the poster child for petulance. "You can't walk down the aisle in your underwear. We have to find something. We've been at this for over two months. There's not much time left."

I sipped my coffee and stared at her. Emily Taylor née Baumgartner was the picture of perfection. Her hair was shiny and manageable, her skin flawless. Her face could easily adorn the cover of *Cosmopolitan*—not that she would be caught dead being associated with a magazine that hyped the *modern woman.* Emily was as old-fashioned as anyone could be. She was also extremely responsible. I'm sure her wedding had been planned out months in advance. I was in a major time crunch now because I'd kept putting things off. I really wanted to be married; I just didn't seem to be able to find the time to get anything accomplished. And now I was in trouble.

A few days ago, Emily'd shown me her wedding pictures. Staring back at me from the white, lace-covered album was the consummate bride. Her dress looked as if it had been tailored especially for her. Emily Baumgartner was born to be a bride.

I, on the other hand, seemed totally unsuited for the role. In every wedding gown I'd tried on, my wild, curly, dark red hair, in contrast to the pale color of the dress, made me look like my head was on fire. Veering away from a white dress didn't seem to be the answer. What if people thought it signified something? I could just see Bertha Pennypacker turn to Marybelle Widdle with a smug smile as I walked down the aisle and whisper, "I knew it all along."

"Maybe I'll just elope," I said glumly. "That way I can wear my green corduroy jumper. Amos likes it."

Emily's light, lilting laugh took a little of the edge off my bad humor. She really was a wonderful friend. I was grateful for her companionship, especially during the times I acted like a spoiled brat. Not many friends can see you at your worst and still find you amusing.

"There's no way you can elope, Ivy," she said. "People in Winter Break love you and Amos. We're not so much like a small town as we are a very large family." She gave me a sympathetic smile. "You know that."

I nodded and forced myself to smile back at her. "You're right. I guess no matter how horrid I look, the most important thing will be that Amos and I are finally married."

She shook her finger at me. "Now, you stop that. You could never look horrid, no matter what you wear. I've never known anyone who had so little sense of her own beauty. I'd love to have red hair and emerald green eyes. I'm so colorless; brown hair and brown eyes. You're. . .you're. . .*vibrant*, Ivy. That's what you are. Vibrant!"

I couldn't help but laugh at her description. "Okay, now you're just getting silly. If you promise to stop, I'll keep looking for the right gown."

She held up her delicate hand. "I swear. No more adjectives."

I took a bite of my tuna salad sandwich and thumbed

through some of the bridal magazines Emily had brought with her. The dresses were beautiful, but most of them were strapless. Winter Break, Kansas, in February wasn't a good time to leave even an inch of skin uncovered unless the lovely shade of *frostbite* goes with your ensemble. I finished the last magazine and pushed it across the table toward her. "I don't see anything here I like."

Emily sighed. "Okay, tell me what kind of dress you envision. Maybe we need to start there and work toward finding *that* gown."

I chewed for a moment, thinking. What *did* I see when I pictured myself walking down the aisle? The answer startled me. "I have no idea, Emily. I've never thought about it."

Emily put her fork down and looked at me like I really had set my head on fire. "Why, Ivy Towers. Every little girl thinks about her wedding day. Are you trying to tell me that you've never dreamed of the perfect wedding?"

"Yes, I've thought about it. I just forgot about the part that had to do with me walking down the aisle, sporting big, pouffy hair while jammed inside a white satin strait jacket. Obviously, that was a mistake."

Emily was quiet for a moment. Then she slowly shook her head. "Most girls only envision themselves on their wedding day. You think about everything else *except* you. You're truly one of a kind." She stared at me quizzically. "I take that back. You do remind me of someone else. Bitty. You two are like peas out of the same pod. Almost every time I'm around you, I see her. It's stronger now than it was when she was alive."

My eyes flushed with tears, and I had to look away. It was a little over a year since my great-aunt Bitty had been murdered inside her bookstore, yet I still felt her presence with me every day. When it came to human beings, there was no greater compliment anyone could pay me than to compare me to her. She was a genuine Christian who loved everyone and had never turned her back on anyone in need. I had no doubt that God would easily be able to say to her, "Well done, good and faithful servant." Now that she was gone, I found myself struggling to carry on her legacy.

Emily scooted her chair next to mine and put her arm around me. "I'm sorry. I didn't mean to upset you."

I patted her hand. "You didn't. I still miss her, you know?"

"I know. I miss her, too."

After a few seconds of silence, I picked up the top magazine on the stack Emily had carted to lunch, and Emily went back to nibbling on her salad. "Okay, let me give this another go. It's only four weeks until the wedding. Unfortunately, that underwear comment you made could become reality."

Emily chuckled. "Well, remember what I said. If you find something but we can't get it here in time, Mama said all we'd have to do is show her a picture and buy some material. She can sew anything."

"That's very sweet, but I wouldn't dream of asking

her to make my gown. It's way too much work."

Emily shook her head, and her expression turned serious. "The truth is, I think you'd be doing her a favor. Ever since Daddy passed away, she seems almost lost. Making your wedding dress might actually help her to feel useful again."

"Really?" I chewed on her comment along with my sandwich. "You know what? If you're sure she'd really want to do it, I'd be thrilled to have her help. I love your mom to pieces, Emily. A dress she made would mean so much more to me than anything I could buy."

"Oh, Ivy. Are you sure?"

I nodded happily. "I'm absolutely certain. I already feel better. Now my dress will be really special."

Emily clapped her hands together. "That was it all along. You wanted a dress that meant something to you. I should have realized that in the first place."

"Don't get too happy. I still have to pick a pattern. We're just preparing to walk into another minefield."

"I have an idea," she said. "Let's find a very basic pattern. Then Mama can customize it for you. That way, you two can work together to make it just the right dress."

"That's a good idea. Now, can we talk about something else? This wedding stuff is starting to get on my nerves."

Emily frowned. "Goodness, you've barely begun. There are a lot of details to planning a wedding. There are the decorations, the flowers, the food, the bridesmaids dresses, the theme, the—"

"Stop!" I spoke louder than I meant to. People sitting around us turned to stare. I lowered my voice. "How in the world am I supposed to plan this entire thing and run the bookstore? I just started buying and selling on the Internet. Orders are coming in steadily now. I can't lose momentum if I want to make the bookstore the kind of success I know it can be."

"I told you I'd help you, Ivy," Emily said quietly. "Don't worry about it. Together we'll—"

"Nonsense," I said, interrupting her again. "You have a new baby to take care of. I appreciate the offer, but you can't give me the kind of help I need."

Emily sighed. "You're probably right. Taking care of Charlie and fixing up the house takes up most of my time."

"Besides, you've already given me the best gift possible."

"What do you mean?"

I smiled at her. "Agreeing to be my maid of honor, silly. There's nothing else you could do that would mean more to me."

"Why, Ivy," she said, her beautiful eyes shining with emotion, "it's an honor."

"Thanks. Now let's change the subject before we both start bawling."

She laughed. "Okay, what would you like to talk about?"

"Tell me what it's like to own a peach orchard."

Emily smiled dreamily. "The orchard is beautiful, and it's wonderful to own all that land. Come spring, we'll see if we can grow peaches. Mama has plans to put up lots of preserves. And now that Buddy and his dad have redone most of the house, I'm really starting to feel at home there."

The Bruenwalder property had some shady history, but after Harvey went to prison, Emily's mother inherited it since she was directly related to Harvey's late wife. She promptly passed the house and land along to Buddy and Emily. The tradition of helping newlyweds was a long-held practice among the Baumgartner clan. The Baumgartners were a force to be reckoned with in Winter Break. Over eighty strong now, they had their own church, First Mennonite, and their family stuck together like glue.

I took another sip of coffee. It was lukewarm. I signaled to the waitress and pointed at my cup. She smiled and went to get the pot. "I'm glad, Emily. It's really a pretty place."

She nodded her agreement. "Thanks. We'd love to have you and Amos over for dinner soon. Sure haven't seen much of him lately."

"These bank robberies are keeping him really busy. The sheriff has him hopping all over the county."

"It's so weird," Emily said. "Why is this guy only robbing banks in Stevens County? It's almost like he's targeting *us*. It feels personal somehow."

"It's not personal. He's hit a couple of banks in

Seward County, too. But you're right. Most of them are certainly close by. He must live somewhere in the area. He's in his comfort zone. Most criminals like to do their dirty deeds in an area they're familiar with."

Emily raised one of her perfectly shaped eyebrows. "There you go again. Are you a bookstore owner or a private detective at heart? Sometimes I can't tell."

I waited until the waitress had warmed up my coffee before I said, "Maybe a little of both. That Nancy Drew gene is hard to ignore."

Emily laughed and looked at her watch. "I think it's time to head back to Winter Break. I need to defrost something for dinner, and you need to work on your wedding list."

I would have objected to the list comment, but it was useless to argue. Making daily lists was another thing I had in common with Aunt Bitty. Then there were the project lists—like the one I'd created for my wedding. Unfortunately, very little had been crossed off.

We paid our ticket and headed back to town. As if crossing an invisible line about a mile before the city limits, the clear roads gave way to blowing and drifting snow. No one knew why Winter Break had snow all winter long while the rest of the state welcomed winter weather only sporadically. It's just the way it was. People in Winter Break accepted it. Funny thing was, you never heard anyone complain. Winter Break seemed to be filled with people who loved winter. A few had moved away to warmer climates, but for the most part, people who were born in Winter Break stayed in Winter Break. Personally, I loved snow. Give me a snowy day over a sunny one anytime. I'd been extremely frustrated while living in Wichita. Snowstorms seemed to drift around the city as if they were afraid to enter. I had nicknamed Wichita "the donut hole of winter."

I may have never had a vision of myself at my wedding, but I'd always known it would be a winter ceremony with twinkling silver lights and fat snowflakes drifting down on me like sparkling confetti. Living in Winter Break gave me a good chance of seeing that dream come true.

I loved life in this special town. A little over six hundred people resided within its borders. A lot of them were farmers. Most of them were wonderful, God-fearing people who shunned life in the big city and were content to live out their days in a place where values still meant something and being a good neighbor was taken for granted. Although Main Street wasn't very long, we actually did have one. Dewey Tater ran the town's only grocery store, Laban's Food-a-Rama. We also had a funeral home, two churches, a restaurant, a post office, a sewing emporium, and a small sheriff's office. In the past year, we'd added a real estate office and an insurance agency. And then, of course, there was the bookstore.

Emily dropped me off in front of Miss Bitty's Bygone Bookstore. I waved good-bye, promising to call her the next day. When I opened the door, the bell above it rang out, welcoming me home. Isaac Holsapple, my assistant, smiled up at me. He was sitting on the floor next to a large stack of books.

"Anything important happen while I was gone?" I hung up my coat and scarf on the coatrack next to the door.

"Not really," he replied. "Miss Hartwell from the library dropped by to see if you had any further donations."

Winter Break was getting ready to welcome its first library. Noel Spivey, a book collector and friend from Denver, had answered my plea for some start-up money that would allow us to open a small, private collection owned and run by the town. After the donation of a building from Dewey, we were working hard to get the library open by early spring. Even though I had a small selection of books that could be borrowed from the bookstore, Winter Break citizens really needed a full range of literary genres to choose from. Hope Hartwell, a young woman who moved to town from Ensign, Kansas, a tiny town outside of Dodge City, had been hired as our librarian. She'd stayed with me for almost a month when she first arrived. Although the city council wasn't able to scrape up as much money as I would have liked, Sarah Johnson, a widow with a large boarding house and an even bigger heart, had offered the young librarian a permanent place to live. She had also invited Hope to share supper with her every evening. Ruby Bird, who ran Ruby's Redbird Café, told Hope she was welcome to eat in the restaurant anytime for free. Winter Break had rallied around the young librarian, making her feel welcome. In some ways, Hope reminded me of Bitty, who came to Winter Break looking for a place to start over after the death of her fiancée. Hope had cared for her beloved grandmother until she passed away. She had no other living relatives.

"I do have some new books for her," I said to Isaac. "Between the residents of Winter Break and the bookstore owners I've contacted through the Internet, we'll have quite a selection by the time we open the doors."

Isaac smiled up at me. "It's an outstanding thing you've done, Miss Ivy. You're making Miss Bitty's dream of making fine literature accessible to everyone in this town come true. She would be very proud of you. I know I am."

The elderly man, who had also been Bitty's assistant before he became mine, had grown to be a very close friend. Although we shared our lives on many levels, I knew that Isaac had been lonely for the kind of intimacy Amos and I couldn't give him. For many years, ever since he'd come to Winter Break, the bookstore had been his whole life. Recently, however, he had expanded his interests a little. Isaac had begun dating Alma Pettibone, Winter Break's postmistress. Alma, a timid woman who hid behind her soap operas, and Isaac, who spent his life with books, had somehow found each other. In my wildest dreams, I would never have paired the two. Isaac was fussy and terminally neat, while Alma was disorganized and forgetful. But somehow they seemed to fulfill a need in each other for companionship.

"I didn't start the library by myself, you know," I said. "The whole town pitched in. Noel and Dewey gave us the foundation we needed."

"You did much more than you give yourself credit for. You lit the fire that got everyone excited about the project. I'm especially happy for the town's children. They will certainly benefit."

I glanced through the stacks of books that Isaac was putting on our bookshelves. A recent purchase from an estate sale had brought us several fine, rare books for our collection, including an early edition of John Bunyan's *Pilgrim's Progress.* I watched as Isaac carefully placed it on the shelf. "Did you hear from Faith today?" I asked.

"No. I'm certain she's over at the library helping Miss Hartwell. She is turning out to be quite a blessing to her."

"Yes, she is. I have to admit that I miss her, though." Faith was a teenager who had attached herself to me during a time of crisis in her life. I'd grown to love her like a daughter, but since Hope had come to town, Faith had thrown herself into helping at the library. It had become a joke around town that our new library was being built on Hope and Faith.

Isaac took off his large, round, tortoiseshell glasses

and pulled a handkerchief from his pocket. "Now, Miss Ivy," he said in a low voice, "you aren't jealous, are you? You're the one who brought the two of them together."

I thought about his question for a moment. "Maybe a little bit," I said slowly. "I know that's terribly immature."

After thoroughly polishing his spectacles, Isaac slipped them back on and stared at me through lenses so thick he reminded me of an owl. "It isn't immature. It's human. Might I suggest that you, as they say, cut yourself a little slack?" He grinned and then went back to inspecting the next book in the stack. "Besides, if you criticize yourself for your actions, it takes all the enjoyment out of it for the rest of us."

I laughed at his last comment. Isaac had recently started to develop a sense of humor. I found this change in his personality very amusing, mostly because it seemed so out of character, but also because he was really quite funny. "I'm so glad that straightening me out is such an important part of life for everyone. I guess I should be happy that I've brought such meaning into your lives."

"It's a dirty job," he sighed. "But someone's got to do it." He smiled at me and then bent over to peruse a list of books that had been cataloged for inclusion into our group of rare books that were for sale. He marked off the last book placed on the shelf then picked up the next book in the stack. "How did your trip to Hugoton go?" he asked. "Did you finally select a dress?"

I had just started to tell him about my lack of success when the front door was pushed open with so much force, I thought the bell was going to fall off. I turned to see Delaphine Shackleford, another new resident of Winter Break, waving her fur-covered arms around like some giant bird trying to take flight. Delaphine was the wife of Barney Shackleford, a salesman for Farm and Field Insurance, a company specializing in rural accounts. Barney had been relocated from Dodge City so he could oversee the company's policyholders in western Kansas. Delaphine, who fancied herself some kind of society queen unfairly banished from her subjects, had made it clear that life in Winter Break was a trial worthy of a true martyr. Pastor Ephraim Taylor, the pastor at Faith Community Church, and Emily's father-in-law, had tried valiantly to involve her in some kind of ministry so she could get her mind off herself and on to something more constructive, but so far, all attempts had failed.

"Ivy Towers!" she called out in her high-pitched voice. "I am here on a mission. I have come to save you!"

Delaphine had a slight southern accent that deepened when she was being dramatic—which was most of the time. No one could figure out just where it came from since she'd grown up in Spearville, a Kansas town about the size of Winter Break. At the present moment, it was as thick as peanut butter.

"Well, actually I've already been saved, Delaphine."

After removing her black fur coat, matching hat, and muff, and carefully inspecting my coat rack for cooties, she hung up her garments and pranced toward the spot where Isaac and I waited.

"Silly, I'm not talking about religious stuff," she declared grandly. "This is something *really* important."

Isaac and I exchanged glances. He looked like he'd just put a lemon in his mouth and was surprised to find out it was sour.

"Delaphine, why don't you have a seat?" I pointed toward the sitting room in the back of the store where an eclectic collection of comfy couches and chairs were arranged for the benefit of those who wanted to snuggle up with a good book and spend the day carried away on the wings of the written word. This special room had also provided the setting for quite a few afternoon naps enjoyed by a variety of Winter Break residents. I had experienced more than one myself. "Can I get you a cup of coffee or a glass of iced tea?"

"No, thank you, dear," she said, clapping her hands together. "I have an idea that has given me all the stimulation I need!"

I followed her to the back of the store after rolling my eyes and folding my hands together as a sign to Isaac that prayer would be appreciated. He just grinned and shrugged his shoulders.

I motioned to a nice burgundy chair. After judging it to be worthy of her royal behind, Delaphine sat down gingerly. I had barely taken the seat next to her when she exploded with enthusiasm. "I am so excited, and you will be, too, when you hear my idea. It's the answer to everything!"

I was fairly certain there were some things in the world that would still not be addressed after her revelation, but I nodded at her, trying to exude some kind of confidence in what I was about to hear. "You've certainly piqued my interest, Delaphine. What is your idea?"

She wiggled her bejeweled fingers at me. "Now, dear, you must call me Dela. All my real friends do."

I smiled. "Okay, Dela. Thank you."

She nodded at me graciously, as if I had just been awarded knighthood. "I heard from Alma Pettibone that you are worried about getting everything done for your wedding. I am here to save the day, Ivy. You don't have to worry about another thing. I am now your *wedding planner*!" She sat back in her chair, a look of triumph on her face. "Now what do you think of that?"

I was dumbstruck. What did I think of that? A wedding planner? Delaphine Shackleford?

"Before you say anything," she said earnestly, "I've done this before—many times. I have a real knack for weddings. I've planned quite a few for my friends. In fact," she lowered her voice to a conspiratorial whisper, "I made all the arrangements for the nuptials of an ex-governor of Kansas. He told me it was the best wedding he'd ever had. Out of all four of them!"

I wasn't sure this was actually a glowing recommendation. Seemed to me that our ex-governor needed to quit worrying about the ceremony and try to figure out what the actual marriage was all about, but still, I could see the excitement in Dela's face—and I *did* need help. . . .

"What would you do, Dela?" I asked. "And what would you charge me?"

"Oh, Ivy," she replied, her tone almost pleading, "I wouldn't charge you anything. I just want to help. I have absolutely nothing to do, and this would make me feel like I'm contributing something." She blinked back tears as she pulled an embroidered handkerchief from her designer handbag and dabbed at her mascara-laden eyes. "Everything here is so different. Sometimes I don't feel like I belong at all. This would help me to feel like a part of Winter Break." She patted her bleached, coiffed hair. "I could bring a little class to this town if you would just give me a chance."

I thought Winter Break's residents were pretty classy already, but I could see her point. I was hoping for a ceremony a little different than the one Amos and I had attended last November. I'm as down-home as the next person, but using your pet pig to carry the ring down the aisle was a little much even for me. Maybe it was the vision of Lulu-belle the pig with a pink pillow tied to her back, or perhaps it was the list I'd started that had almost nothing crossed off, but I found myself nodding at Dela. This really *could* be the answer to my problems. Someone else could worry about all the wedding details while I concentrated on the bookstore. And, Dela could make some new friends in the bargain. It sounded like the perfect solution.

What could possibly go wrong?

"You did what? Are you out of your mind?"

Amos's reaction wasn't really what I'd been hoping for. I'd been congratulating myself all day for being very clever. Dela Shackleford was ecstatic and already hard at work. She'd called me just before I left for dinner, claiming to have already come up with several "enchanting" ideas for the wedding. We had an appointment in the morning to go over them.

"I don't think you need to be so negative," I said crossly, taking a bite of my fruit salad while Amos stuck a forkful of Ruby's Monday night special in his mouth. Monday was chicken-fried steak and mashed potatoes, both smothered in thick chicken gravy. After much cajoling, Ruby had finally added some healthy dishes to the choices at Ruby's Redbird Café, the only restaurant in Winter Break. Her long-lost son, Bert, had returned to town last summer and was helping her run things. His influence had certainly added some support to my campaign for less saturated fat on the menu. Together, Bert and I convinced Ruby that fruit didn't have to be served in a pie and vegetables didn't exist just so they could be breaded and fried in lard. My concern for Dewey Tater's diabetes and my waistline had instigated my crusade, but now, many of Winter Break's citizens were ordering salads, steamed vegetables, whole grains, and fresh fruits. These pioneers would most likely never be in the majority, but it did my heart good to know that at least some of our residents might actually enjoy the feeling of unclogged arteries for once. However, as in most fierce battles, I had been forced to concede one thing: Ruby's Redbird Burgers. They were less like food and more like a drug happily ingested by the entire population of Winter Break. Her burgers were heaven on a bun. That is if heaven had fried meat, cheddar cheese, and a secret ingredient that most Winter Break residents would give their firstborn for. I'd accepted the healthy menu additions as a victory and hadn't even attempted to attack the Holy Grail of Ruby's Redbird Café. They say that wisdom is knowing how to pick your battles.

After stuffing a couple of large bites of mashed potatoes in his mouth, Amos swallowed, put his fork down, and gaped at me. "I'm not being negative, Ivy. But Delaphine Shackleford is nuts. She's called me out to her place at least a dozen times since she and Barney moved here. She's always *hearing* something or *seeing* something outside her house. Once I found Newton Widdle's cow wandering around on their property and another time she swore someone was calling her name. It was a barn owl in the tree next to their bedroom window. She just needs to understand that living in the country isn't the same thing as living in the city. She actually asked me once if I would spend the night in my car and keep a watch over her place. I tried to explain that I work for the sheriff in Hugoton and that just because I live here doesn't mean I'm available to her day and night."

I jabbed a juicy, sweet piece of melon with my fork. Ruby had canned and frozen lots of fruit for the winter. Even though I knew she used some sugar in the process, the result was still yummy and better for me than the rest of the cholesterol-laden menu.

"It's hard for people to understand, Amos," I said. "You have an office here. People think they can call you whenever they need help."

"In most situations, they can. I just have to clear it through the sheriff. I'm certain he wouldn't want me staking out Dela's house on a whim." He frowned and stared down at his food. "Anyway, that office isn't mine. It was put here for any deputy who needed a place to park themselves if they couldn't get to Hugoton for some reason. It's not my fault that none of the other deputies ever come to Winter Break."

He sounded sincere, but I knew he viewed the small space as his own. God help any deputy sheriff who came to town and expected to be welcomed into that office with open arms.

"Look, I really need help with the wedding. You're out chasing bank robbers, and I'm trying to run the bookstore. I need Dela and she needs me. You know how hard it's been for her to adjust to life here."

Amos snorted. "Delaphine Shackleford would have a hard time adjusting wherever she went. She's a self-centered woman who is only interested in things that benefit *her*. She's getting something she wants out of helping you. I'm afraid you'll discover that our wedding is not her top priority."

I set my fork down. "Amos Parker. Whatever happened to not judging people? Did you conveniently forget what the Bible says?" I gave him my most angelic look. "'Do not judge, or you too will be judged. . .and with the measure you use, it will be measured to you.'"

"Okay, Miss Holier-Than-Thou. You can take a break." He waved his knife at me. "I seem to remember a few comments you made about Bertha Pennypacker last week. Let's see, what was it? You called her a nosy—"

"That's enough," I interrupted. "Two wrongs don't make a right. Besides, I don't think you should be bringing up things from the past. It's not very Christian."

Amos laughed and stabbed another piece of steak. "Marriage to you is certainly going to be interesting. You're something else, you know that?"

"Well, anyway," I said, "I'm willing to try this. From what I've heard, Barney's company intends for him to be here awhile. He and Dela need to make some friends."

Amos quit chewing and stared at me, his boyish face twisted with concern. "You don't want anyone to be unhappy, do you? The thing that worries me is that the one person you don't think about is yourself. I'm just trying to look after you." He reached over, took my chin in his hand, and stared into my eyes. "I intend to spend the rest of my life doing that."

I kissed him—even with the smell of chicken-fried steak on his breath. "Thank you. I look forward to it. But right now I need you to give Dela a chance. Will you do that, please? For me?"

He leaned back in his seat and let out a sigh of resignation. "Okay, Ivy. Let Delaphine Shackleford plan the wedding. But if this doesn't work. . ."

"It will, Amos. I'm sure it will." The words sounded good when I said them, but there was a little niggling twinge of worry inside my gut. I sent a silent prayer heavenward. If this turned out badly, I was going to be eating something besides wedding cake. A heaping dish of crow wasn't going to go down as easily.

"Have you seen that dog again?" Amos asked, thankfully changing the subject. A stray dog had started showing up around my house. Although he was dirty and his hair was matted, I was pretty sure he was a border collie. Black and white, with an intelligent face, he would prowl around the lake, coming close to the house. But when I called him or got within a few feet of him, he would run away. "He was sitting near the lake when I left this morning."

"Don't feed him, Ivy. He could be dangerous. There's no way to know how long he's been running loose."

It was a sad fact of life that people who wanted to

get rid of their pets would sometimes dump them in rural areas. Winter Break had certainly seen its share of stray dogs. Unfortunately, after awhile many of them would start acting wild and running in packs. Once that started, it was almost impossible to tame them again.

"He's always by himself, Amos. There aren't any dogs with him. Maybe he'll learn to trust me."

He shook his head. "I really don't want you putting yourself in danger. He might be vicious. He could even have rabies. Please stay away from him."

I smiled, but I didn't say anything. I'd been putting food and water out for him every day for a week. I couldn't turn my back on him now. He had the saddest eyes I'd ever seen. He'd probably watched his family drive away without him, abandoning him to a life of loneliness and desperation. Rejection hurt, especially when you couldn't understand what was happening.

I tried to push my concerns about the dog away for a while so I could concentrate on finishing my meal. Amos launched into a story about chasing down some guy who'd been writing bad checks in Hugoton. I tried to listen, but my thoughts kept bouncing back and forth between the abandoned dog and Dela. I wasn't sure which one worried me most.

On the way home, Amos warned me once again about the dog. I wondered if my silence gave me away, but I couldn't just walk away from the pitiful animal—even if I wanted to. And I didn't. After a good-night kiss and a reminder about an important meeting the next day, I said good-bye and went inside my house. After Amos left, I checked outside, but I didn't see the dog anywhere.

Tuesday morning I had breakfast with Dewey Tater, just like every weekday morning. As much as I enjoyed our breakfasts, I found myself rushing through it. Dela was bringing over her wedding ideas, and I was finally starting to get excited. I felt a little guilty about Dewey. He was a good friend. He had been engaged to marry Bitty before she died. They'd shared breakfast together every day before they each opened the doors to their respective businesses. Although I'd hoped he'd develop another special relationship, at almost eighty years old, Dewey wasn't interested. "Bitty was the love of my life," he'd declared more than once. "Guess I'll just stop now while I'm ahead." And that was it. He believed he would be with Bitty again someday, and he didn't want any other female "mucking up" his reunion. "How would I explain that to Bitty?" he'd grumble when I tried to encourage him to find a new lady friend. I'd finally given up. Someday Dewey would breathe his last. It would be a sad day for me, but I knew in my heart that as soon as Dewey closed his eyes on this earth, he'd open them in heaven, and Bitty would be waiting there to welcome him home.

About eight thirty, Dewey ambled out of the bookstore so he could open Laban's Food-a-Rama to the public. I cleaned up our breakfast dishes and made another pot of coffee in the small kitchen upstairs where I'd lived when I first came to Winter Break. It had been Bitty's apartment then mine. Now that I lived in my dream house by the lake, I'd turned the apartment into a storage area for books and other things. However, I kept the kitchen stocked so I could make something to eat without going all the way home or being forced to eat at Ruby's every day. I put some bagels and cream cheese on a plate and carried everything downstairs to the sitting room. I'd just reset the table when Dela came flying through the front door.

"Ivy?" she sang out in her southern-tinged falsetto. "Ivy Towers! Your wedding guru has arrived!"

I waved at her. "I'm back here, Dela."

She bounced back to where I stood waiting. She looked like a skinny version of Mrs. Claus. She wore a red velvet dress with white fur around the wrists and neck. Perched on her ash blond head was a white fur hat, and on her feet were knee-high black leather boots. I glanced down at my jeans and sweater. I was suddenly glad that I'd already formulated a plan for my wedding dress. I wasn't certain Dela and I had the same taste in clothes.

I motioned toward the table. "Let's sit here, Dela, so we'll have plenty of room. Would you like some coffee?"

She pulled out a chair and sat down, pushing the food tray out of her way. Then she took a large folder from her attaché case. She raised her eyebrows and looked at the coffeepot in my hand. "I'm only drinking Peruvian Organic now. I don't suppose. . ."

I set the pot down. "No. It's just plain American coffee."

She raised her nose in the air just a smidgen. Not so much so that I could say she was actually rude, but just enough so that I knew she wouldn't be caught dead drinking good old Folgers.

"What about a bagel?" Silly me, not willing to quit while I was behind.

Dela looked at the tray I'd prepared as if I were serving roadkill. "No, nothing for me, thank you," she said in an overly polite tone.

Well, things were certainly starting off well. The inside of my stomach was beginning to feel like the cast of Riverdance had taken up residence. What was I getting into? I poured myself a cup of coffee and moved the food tray out of the way. Dela, seemingly relieved to be distanced from my low-class hillbilly brunch, spread her papers out in front of us.

"Now, dear," she said in an excited voice, "I have some of the most wonderful ideas for your wedding. Wait until you hear them! First of all, we need to establish a theme. It should be something new and innovative. You know—something avant-garde!"

Her fake southern accent, combined with an attempt at a French phrase, was incredibly comical. I kept my mouth shut tight so as not to giggle and offend her.

"Oh, I'm sorry," she said. "Avant-garde means—"

"I know what it means, Dela," I interrupted, feeling my face flush. "Let's just look at your ideas, okay?" My momentary attack of humor had turned quickly into irritation. My clipped response sounded harsh, even though I hadn't planned it.

Dela's smile disappeared. She reached over and patted my knee with her perfectly trimmed fingers. "I'm sorry, honey," she said softly. "I get a little carried away sometimes. I don't mean anything by it." Her brightly polished nails looked like drops of blood against my jeans. They matched the large gold and ruby-red ring she wore on her right hand. On her left, she supported a sparkling wedding ring set that must have cost a pretty penny. A large rhinestone bracelet slid down her wrist and onto her hand. It seemed too big for her, but almost everything about Dela was larger than life. Her clothes, her jewelry, her accent, and her attitude. I couldn't begin to guess how many pieces of jewelry she owned. A few of the women at church had remarked that she changed her jewelry more than her clothes, sometimes sporting as many as three different sets a day.

And I hadn't meant to hurt her feelings. My goal was to encourage her. "I'm sorry, Dela. Really. I guess I'm just a little nervous about getting everything done in time for the wedding."

She immediately brightened up. "I understand. I'm here to make everything better. Now let's take a look at my ideas."

She pulled out several pictures and laid them in front of me. The first one showed a woman in a short white wedding dress with an open bodice in the shape of a heart. I could almost see her navel. The bridesmaids were in pink velvet mini-dresses with puffy sleeves. They looked decidedly grim. I certainly couldn't blame them.

"Isn't this lovely?" Dela gushed. "It's all built around a Valentine's Day theme." She picked up her notebook and began to read. "The chapel will be decorated with red roses and calla lilies. Red hearts will be everywhere; hanging from the ceiling, on the walls, even red hearts set down like footsteps up to the altar. Two children will walk down the aisle, throwing red rose petals. They will be dressed like cherubs." She sighed and put her hand to her chest as if trying to reign in her utter excitement. "Amos will wear a classic black tuxedo with a red tie and cummerbund. Your bridal bouquet will be red roses in the shape of a heart. Of course, you will walk down the aisle to Mendelssohn's 'Wedding March,' but there will be other music as well. I suggest "'Sheep May Safely Graze'" by Bach or "'Dance of the Blessed Spirits'" by Glück." She waved her hand dismissively. "Of course, some people want Canon in D by Pachelbel. It's become rather pedestrian, but it's your wedding. We can include it if you wish. And the food. . ." At this she broke out in a girlish giggle. "In keeping with our romantic theme, we'll have an oyster bar, asparagus, chicken with mole sauce, and a chocolate fountain with strawberries and bananas for dipping."

I should have said something right after seeing the hideous bridesmaid dresses and the peek-a-boo wedding gown, but somehow I seemed to have lost the ability to speak. As it was, I had to try several times to get anything coherent out of my mouth. "But. . .I can't. . . are you serious. . .I mean. . ." Finally, I stopped and took another run at it. "I don't know where to start, Dela," I said. I didn't want to cause her any further emotional distress, but I was somewhat manic by then. "This just isn't me. And I don't want any red hearts at my wedding, even if it is Valentine's Day."

Those red hearts hanging everywhere reminded me of second grade when we all made big red hearts out of construction paper and decorated them. Some of them were to take home to our parents, and some of them were for classmates. Miss Curtis, our teacher, put bags with our names on them on the large corkboard on the wall. We had just moved to the district and I didn't know any of the kids very well. I was the only child in class who didn't get a valentine.

"Well, maybe if we cut down the number—"

"No, Dela. No red hearts. None. I'm sorry."

She tried to interrupt me, but I raised my hand up and put it near her face.

"No red hearts. Anywhere. At all. Ever. Never."

She clamped her mouth shut so tightly, it was just a thin line surrounded by white. Her eyes narrowed with annoyance but to her credit, she stayed quiet.

"And I'm not showing my stomach—or anything

else. Besides, Inez Baumgartner is making my dress. That's already taken care of. And Amos already has his tux picked out."

"Well, it would have been nice if you'd told me about the wedding clothes before I spent all this time looking through gowns and tuxedos," she said, her words quick and clipped.

"I'm sorry," I said, trying my best to smooth things over now that the blood was once again flowing to my brain. "You're right."

"Is there anything else I should know?" She raised one eyebrow and stared at me coldly.

"I don't know. I really don't have anything specific in mind, but there are a few things that are important to me." This was turning out badly, and I really wanted it to work. For me and for Dela. I thought for a moment while she glared at me. I decided to swallow my pride. It was either that or confess to Amos that I'd made a mistake. I took the easier route. "I haven't been fair to you, Dela. I should have told you about my dress and Amos's tuxedo before you put so much time into this. I'm so sorry. I just didn't think about it."

Dela didn't respond, but her expression softened a little.

"I want things to be tasteful and simple. And I'd like a winter theme. I want to be married in the church, but I want the reception at my house." I shook my head. "I think that's about it."

"First of all," Dela said, her words like small,

sharp blasts of machine gun fire, "anything *I* do will be tasteful."

I glanced at the poor pink bridesmaids, their humiliation captured forever in a glossy eight-by-ten. Dela and I definitely had different ideas of what "tasteful" meant.

"Secondly," she continued, "you absolutely cannot have the reception at your house."

If the hearts and flowers wedding theme hadn't convinced me that I'd made a terrible error in judgment, Dela's declaration cemented it. "What do you mean?" I said slowly enough so she could understand me. "I'm having the reception at my house."

She sat back in her chair with her mouth open in horror. "I have already planned for it in the community room at the church, and I simply can't rework it." She crossed her arms and gazed at me defiantly. "Besides, I've already booked it."

I held my breath and silently counted to ten—something my father had taught me to do when dealing with my mother. When I reached nine, I took a deep breath. "Dela, I really appreciate your help with my wedding, but the reception is going to be at my house. Ruby and Bert are going to do the cooking. I am quite open to your suggestions about the wedding and even the reception, but please check with me before booking anything else, okay?"

Dela started grabbing things from the table, pushing papers together in a huff. "I can't work like this," she declared.

My first reaction was sheer joy. She was quitting. I was free! But then she started to cry. I have to admit that a brief battle ensued inside me. If I let her walk out now, my life would be much easier, and I could prevent looming disaster. Instead, I found myself saying, "I'm sorry, Dela. Please let me see your other ideas. Just because I didn't like that one, it doesn't mean I won't like something else."

There were three reasons I said what I did. Number one: Dela was lonely and needed to feel connected to her new community. Number two: I was too stubborn to tell Amos he was right all along. And number three: I knew what my aunt Bitty would have done in the same circumstances. She would have considered Dela's feelings more important than her wedding plans. There may have been a fourth reason that had to do with a slight case of insanity, but I didn't have time to come up with any other explanations for my behavior.

Dela quit maniacally shuffling papers around and grabbed her designer handbag. She took out a hanky and wiped her eyes. "I don't know," she said between high-pitched hiccups. "I've never been treated like this before. Everyone else loves my ideas. The ex-governor told me that I'd created the wedding to end all weddings." She sniffed a few times then blew her nose. "And they're still together, I might add."

I wasn't really surprised. The poor man probably couldn't face another Dela Shackleford wedding. "I'm sure it's just me, Dela. Let's look over your other proposals. I'll bet there's something here that will be absolutely perfect."

She put her handkerchief back in her purse. "I do have a couple of other ideas. . ."

"I'd love to see them." I was praying as hard as I could without looking like I was storming heaven. It wasn't easy. There was a little, invisible version of myself on the inside, jumping up and down and yelling as loudly as possible, asking God if He could drop everything for just a few seconds and save me from this imminent wedding nightmare.

Dela searched through her stack and pulled out another folder. "Now, these pictures are of *my* wedding."

She paused and looked up toward the ceiling. I almost followed her gaze to see what was so interesting but stopped myself just in time.

"It was the most beautiful wedding I've ever seen," she said dreamily. "Why, people in Dodge City didn't know what to think." She kept staring heavenward for several seconds. Finally, she lowered her head and smiled at me. "Do you know that every single person who attended said the same thing?"

"And what was that, Dela?"

"That they'd never seen anything like it." She shook her head slowly. "And now I am going to do the same thing for you."

That little invisible person jumping up and down inside of me sat down with a *thunk*. Obviously this was one of God's busier days.

In my worst imagination, I wasn't prepared for what awaited me. The first thing I saw was a picture of Dela decked out in a red silk gown with a large yellow dragon splayed across the front. On her head she wore some kind of gold crown with a red veil. Short, stocky Barney was stuffed into a red tux with a matching yellow dragon on the jacket front. He looked like one of those chubby, plastic boy dolls you find in gift stores that has been draped in a cheap Chinese costume. The next picture was a shot of the bridesmaids and the groomsmen. It wasn't any better. They were all dressed in yellow satin. The bridesmaids had red sashes around their middles that made them look decidedly frumpy and overweight, and they clutched sandalwood fans in their hands. One of the women held hers up to her face. Although she was trying hard to make the gesture look playful, I suspect she was hoping it might keep her from having to leave town and create a whole new identity. The men all wore shiny yellow tuxedos with red accents. That's all that needs to be said about that.

The next several pictures showed the inside of the church. Lanterns hung from every available space. Red banners with gold Chinese figures were draped around the room. And hanging behind the stage was a large papier-mâché dragon. Dela tried to push another picture in front of me, but I couldn't take my eyes off that dragon for some reason. I wanted to look away—but I couldn't.

When I finally gazed down at the last picture, I saw

the aisles in the church decorated with Chinese fans and orchids. It was the only part of the monstrosity I could say something positive about. "I. . .I like what you did here. The orchids are lovely."

Dela clapped her hands together with delight. "I knew you'd love this. With your parents being missionaries in China and all. . ."

I was fairly certain my parents would not only hate this, they would most probably disown me if they ever saw this make-believe Chinese monstrosity. I thought fast. "You know, Dela, it's very thoughtful of you to think of my parents, but the truth is, I think they'd rather not see a Chinese wedding. I mean, they've been in China a long time now. I think they are expecting something more. . .American. Do you understand?" I wasn't sure how she could possibly understand since it didn't even make sense to me, but I smiled like what I'd said was perfectly logical.

Dela stared at me with narrowed eyes. "Well, I don't know. . ." She grabbed the attaché case from under the table. "I brought some favors with me for you to look at." She dumped several things out in front of me. "These are napkin rings for the reception. They're in the shape of fortune cookies. And here are some paper parasols." She reached further inside the bag. "Now these are really special." She pulled out a box and set it in front of me. "Every guest will get a set of chopsticks with the bride and groom's names on them. Of course, those will be wooden. But this set is for you and Amos." She opened the box to reveal a set of long, bronze chopsticks with pointed ends. Engraved on one side were the names *Delaphine and Barney Shackleford—May 6th, 1986.* She took them out of the box and handed them to me.

I was startled to hear someone behind me clear his throat. Fearful that it was Amos, I turned around and was relieved to find Isaac standing just to the left of my chair.

"Sorry to disturb you," he said. "I'm getting ready to start work. Any special instructions?"

I shook my head, numb with embarrassment. I could tell by the look on his face that he found my predicament extremely entertaining. I was just as aware that he knew exactly what needed to be done. He'd just wanted to get a gander at those awful pictures. He was looking for ammunition—something he could tease me about. This would certainly keep him equipped for quite some time.

After he left, Dela leaned in close to me. "Why don't you give this some thought, Ivy? If you really think your parents wouldn't like it, that's okay." She sighed. "To be honest, I doubt that the magic of this event could ever be duplicated. I struggled with even showing this to you. I don't want you and Amos to feel that you have to try to live up to a standard that's. . . well, out of your reach." She shot me a look of pity that made me want to tell her what I really thought of her wonderful wedding—but I didn't.

"You're absolutely right. We would probably come off as poor imitations. I hate to do anything that might cast a bad light on your unique event."

I seemed to hit the right nerve. Dela nodded and began gathering up the mementos of her nightmarish Chinese ceremony. I handed her the chopsticks and sent a quick prayer of thanks to God along with my apologies for ever doubting Him. I hoped that Dela interpreted my sigh of relief as a sign of my great disappointment.

After fiddling with what seemed to be a defective clasp on the box that held the chopsticks, she finally put it into her purse. "I've got to have Barney fix that fastener before I lose something that can't possibly be replaced."

My guess was that whoever came up with the engraved chopsticks idea was probably no longer in business. Therefore, Dela's observation had some real merit.

"I do have one more idea that might be more your style," she purred.

I seriously doubted that Dela and I would ever have the same kind of style, but to my surprise, when she opened the final notebook in her case, the results were surprising. "This is a fairytale wedding," Dela said. "It lacks the color and verve of my wedding, but I think there's something quite magical about it."

The bride's gown was ivory satin with a beaded bodice. Small rhinestones were scattered throughout the white beads, giving the dress a lovely shimmer. The sleeves were long, made out of lace, and the bride held a white winter muff. Instead of a long veil, a small, sparkly band threaded through her hair.

The bridesmaids wore simple dresses, touched with a hint of dusky grey. Although they were sleeveless, each girl had a matching shawl draped around her shoulders.

The church was decorated with small, twinkling lights and crystal snowflakes that hung from the ceiling. White orchids graced the platform with silver candlesticks.

"Why, Dela," I said. "This is beautiful. I think you've captured the winter look I want."

The smile on Dela's face told me she was pleased. However, she couldn't resist one last dig. "I guess the other weddings were just a little too imaginative for you," she said, patting my hand. Although her tone was obviously patronizing, I was just happy that this whole thing hadn't blown up in my face. Telling Amos that accepting Dela's help hadn't been the disaster he'd anticipated almost made viewing Barney Shackleford in a red satin tux worth it. Almost.

"Can I have this picture of the wedding dress?" I asked. "I'd like to show it to Inez. It can be our guide."

"Absolutely," she said. "Why don't you keep this folder? You can go over everything and make a list of any changes. I will need to meet with you again in a couple of days so we can start ordering our supplies." She handed me the folder. "What kind of budget are we talking about, dear?"

I mentioned a figure Amos and I had agreed on. At first, we'd decided that we didn't want my parents to help with the cost of the wedding. As missionaries, we felt their finances should be protected. My dad had sent us a check anyway, insisting that helping us was a joy and reminding me that they actually did have money of their own, thank you. We applied his check along with what we believed we could afford, and came up with a sum we felt was completely sufficient for our needs. Dela's reaction made it evident that our budget would seriously constrain her creativity.

"Oh, my," she said, a frown darkening her face. "We'll have to do better than that. I can't even begin to pull this wedding off for that much. You'll have to at least double your budget."

"Dela, I appreciate everything you're doing, but that's the amount we have to spend. Period. If we can't do it, we can't do it. I appreciate your help anyway." I smiled at her and stood up, sticking out my hand. My bluff worked, just as I knew it would.

"Well, I'll just have to find some way to pull it off," she said, shaking her head and ignoring my extended digits. "I am the kind of person who likes challenges. This certainly will test my mettle." She stared up at me, determination on her face. I was now Delaphine Shackleford's pet project. She stood up. "I will need to see your house now," she said matter-of-factly. "If I am to plan the reception there, I must see what I'm working with." The look of resignation on her face conveyed her fears that I most probably lived in a van by the river. I wondered what she would think when she saw my Queen Anne-style Victorian house next to Lake Winter Break. It was a gorgeous house, the prettiest in Winter Break.

"I'm sorry, but as you can see, I'm working right now. I just can't spare the time. Why don't we make an appointment for another day?"

Dela's smile froze on her face. "Pardon me, honey," she said icily, her pseudo-southern accent as thick as sorghum, "but my time is important, too. I've taken the morning off so I can help you. I think the least you can do is to treat my offer of free services with respect, don't you?"

"Excuse me." Isaac appeared behind us, supposedly looking for something on a shelf near the sitting room. "I've got everything under control, Miss Ivy. Why don't you go ahead and take Mrs. Shackleford to your house? I'll watch the store."

His smile looked sincere, but I could see the twinkle in his eye. "Well, thank you so much, Isaac," I said. "I will certainly return the favor to you at an appropriate moment in the future."

He swept his arm in front of him with a slight bow. "I appreciate that," he said with a grin. "I will be watching for it most carefully."

I glared at him as I tagged along behind Dela to the front door. She followed me over to my house. Once we got there, it took her over an hour to inspect my living room, dining room, and kitchen. Although she made clucking noises every couple of minutes, in the end, she grudgingly admitted that she could probably pull off an acceptable reception there. The dining room had large windows and French doors that faced Lake Winter Break. Dela decided that this feature could be used to our advantage.

"I have all kinds of ideas," she told me. "But I want some time to sketch them out, and I have an errand in town I must take care of. Why don't I stop by tomorrow and we can discuss them?"

I agreed to meet her the next day at the bookstore, and after an odd kiss near my cheek that never actually touched my face, she left. Since it was almost noon, I decided to have lunch before I went back to work. I fixed a sandwich, sat at the dining room table, and gazed out at Lake Winter Break. Since it was thoroughly frozen over, I'd raised the yellow flag on a pole near the lake. Cecil Biddle, who had once owned my house, had installed the pole when I was a kid as a way to let folks in Winter Break know that the lake was safe for skating. On the weekends it was full of children. I loved to watch them from my window. This was probably my favorite place in the house to sit and read my Bible, pray, or just daydream. It gave me a sense of peace.

I'd just finished my sandwich when I saw the dog. He was skulking around the backyard deck. The pan of food I'd set out for him was still a little over half full, so he wasn't hungry. I got the feeling he was curious. I didn't want to spook him again, so I stayed where I was. After a few minutes he looked my way, but this time he stood still and stared at me. His expression was still melancholy, but for the first time, he also looked inquisitive—as if he were trying to figure me out. Finally, he turned and ran back through the trees that surrounded one side of the lake.

The past few weeks had been pretty cold, and we were set for another snowstorm. I couldn't help but worry about him. But along with concern for the dog, I felt something else stirring inside me. Something on a deeper level. I remembered what Aunt Bitty told me once about what she used to call "God's fire alarm." "When God rings that fire alarm inside you," she'd say, "it means you better pay attention. Something somewhere needs a dose of prayer."

I happened to glance up at the clock on the wall. It was later than I'd thought. I prayed quietly while I cleaned up the kitchen and put the food away, but I could swear that alarm got even louder.

I finished up my work at the bookstore and rushed home. After a quick dinner and a change of clothes, I headed to the church. The Winter Break City Council, led by Mayor Dewey Tater, had called a special meeting for seven o'clock. He planned to announce his selection of citizens to serve as the new library's advisory board. I knew my name was on the list, but for the most part, Dewey had kept his final selections to himself. He'd asked my opinion about what qualities I thought were important for a library board member, but he didn't mention any names. I knew he took his role as Winter Break's mayor seriously, even though there wasn't much for him to do. City council meetings were usually boring affairs where the placement of street signs and trash Dumpsters topped the agenda. However, the whole town was excited about the library, and quite a few people had expressed a desire to be on the board. Tonight promised to hold some actual excitement.

When I arrived, the meeting had just started. I wasn't the least bit surprised to see Dela sitting on the front row, still dressed in her red velvet and fur outfit. She was determined to be the cream of society wherever she was—even if it was in Winter Break, Kansas.

Alma Pettibone, who served not only as our postmistress but also as the city clerk, called the meeting to order. Elmer Buskins, owner of Buskins Funeral Home, had just moved to have the minutes from the last meeting approved, when Amos came in the door and scooted into the chair next to me. He slid off his parka and hung it on the back of the chair. Then he kissed me on the cheek. I grabbed his hand and held it while Mort Benniker seconded the motion. I noticed that one of the council seats at the table was empty. J.D. Feldhammer was missing. J.D. and his wife, Ina Mae, had only lived in Winter Break for about six months. He was a real estate agent who had moved here from Liberal, Kansas. He handled a lot of farm properties and had put together the deal for my home. He'd been recommended to Cecil and Marion Biddle, who'd sold the house to Amos as a surprise for me. When Ina Mae needed to be close to her sickly mother who lived in Hugoton, J.D. had purchased Lester Simmons's property. Lester's house had been vacant for quite a while, and rumor had it that J.D. got it for a really good price. He seemed very happy here and was well liked by everyone who had gotten to know him. I liked Ina Mae, too, although she was painfully shy. It had taken awhile for me to get past her reserved persona, but now she was in the habit of dropping by the bookstore every few days to visit and have a cup of coffee. I looked through the crowd and spotted her sitting by herself near the back of the room. Because of J.D.'s business, Ina Mae often needed a ride to church or to events like this evening's meeting. I made a mental note to check with her before we left to see if she had a way home.

I focused my attention back to Dewey, who announced the reason for tonight's meeting. "We're here to set up a board for the library," he said, trying to speak loudly enough for everyone to hear. "As you all probably know, we asked for a letter from anyone interested in being a part of the board, with an explanation as to why you think you are qualified for this position. I was asked to read those letters then recommend some folks for the board, subject to the council's approval." He pulled his glasses out of his pocket and perched them on his nose. "After a careful review, I am recommending the following people for the board." He picked up a piece of paper from the table and began to read. "Ivy Towers, Isaac Holsapple, Bev Taylor, Bertha Pennypacker, Evan Baumgartner, and Delaphine Shackleford."

I was horrified. Dewey had nominated Bertha Pennypacker and Dela? He knew how difficult they were to get along with. What was he thinking? I was happy to know that I would be serving with Isaac, and Bev Taylor, Pastor Taylor's wife. And Evan Baumgartner, one of the teachers from the grade school in Hugoton, was a good choice. But Bertha and Dela?

"I didn't see that coming," Amos whispered to me.

I'm sure the lack of blood in my face indicated my agreement, but I didn't say anything. I was afraid to.

Bubba Weber seconded Dewey's nominations and Dewey called for a vote. His list was passed unanimously. I wanted to cry. My dreams of a library board working together for the good of the community seemed lost, as well as my election as board president. Bertha, the town's gossip, had taken a dislike to me right after I came to Winter Break. Dewey told me that she had always been jealous of Bitty and had transferred her attitude on to me. Of course, the fact that I'd helped Amos break up her husband's cow-stealing ring hadn't helped anything. Good old Delbert was now cooling his heels in the Hutchinson Correctional Facility, and Bertha hated me even more.

After encouraging the board to meet and start writing out its goals and then present them to the city council at their next regular assembly, the meeting was dismissed. Ruby had set up a table with desserts and coffee. People made a beeline for it, leaving me and Amos standing in the back of the room.

"Let's go," I hissed. "I'm so mad I could spit nails."

Amos looked surprised. "Why are you upset? I thought you wanted to be on the board."

I stared at him in amazement. "You think I'm happy that Dewey picked Bertha and Dela? What in the world makes them suitable to serve on a library board?" I shook my head. "Dewey must have lost his mind. We'll never get anything accomplished if we have to kowtow to those two prima donnas."

"Ivy Towers," someone said from behind me, "maybe we should just let the entire council go and put you in charge of everything."

I turned around to find Dewey standing there. To say I was mortified was an understatement. "I—I—I. . ."

was all that would come out of my mouth.

"You might be surprised to find out that Bertha Pennypacker's mother was a librarian, and that she was practically raised in a library. And you might also be surprised to learn that Delaphine Shackleford was on the Dodge City Library Board. She has just the kind of experience we need."

I wanted to say that she probably only served because it nicely filled out her social calendar, but I'd already said too much. I decided to cut my losses and shut up.

Dewey looked at me with an expression I'd never seen on his face before: disappointment. Then he said the one thing that had the power to make me feel worse than I already did. "Your aunt Bitty would be ashamed of you right now. I don't remember her ever saying an unkind word about anyone."

With that, he turned and walked away, leaving me to stand there with my bad attitude hanging out for all the world to see. People were beginning to drift around the room—their plates stacked high with Ruby's scrumptious desserts. I wasn't certain who'd heard Dewey scold me, but I was mortified. Almost everyone I knew was at the meeting.

"Let's go," I said to Amos. I could feel tears sting my eyelids, and I had no intention of blubbering in front of the city council and my new library board pals.

Before he had a chance to respond, a shrill voice cut through the sound of regular conversation in the room. "Hello there, Ivy! Who would have thought you and I would be serving on the same board!" Dela's southern screech shot through the room like an errant bullet. "I'm so excited to know that we will be working together on *two* important projects." She linked her arm through mine like we were best friends. "And I want you to know that I will be happy to serve as board president since I have so much experience."

Her smile had a touch of triumph in it. I wondered if she'd already been campaigning for the position. As if on cue, Bertha Pennypacker sidled up next to her. "Oh, Dela," she said in syrupy tones, "you would make the perfect president. Don't you think so, Ivy?"

I just nodded since I didn't trust myself enough to open my mouth. Bertha took this as a vote of confidence. "Then I'm sure you'll convince the other members of the board to vote for our dear Dela, won't you?"

Bertha, in her cheap dress and home perm, was preening for attention from someone who probably saw her only as a means to an end. Curiously, I found myself feeling rather sorry for her. Having a husband in prison certainly couldn't be a boost to her self-esteem.

"We'll see, Bertha," I said. "Why don't we wait and discuss it at our first meeting? Can we set a time for it now?"

"Why, Ivy," Dela simpered. "I think that's a wonderful idea. When should we meet? What about tomorrow night?"

"That's a church night," I said, wondering if she already knew that. "What about Thursday night? We could meet at the bookstore."

"Hmmm," Dela said. "I suppose we could get together there, but why don't you let me bring the hors d'oeuvres? I have some recipes that would be, uh, appropriate."

I was thinking about telling her just what she could do with her "appropriate" hors d'oeuvres, but I already had Dewey mad at me. Creating more strife would only make things worse.

I returned her saccharine smile with one of my own. Amos's lopsided grin told me I probably looked more constipated than amused. "Thank you, Dela. That's very nice of you. Thursday night it is. We'll need to let the others know."

"Bertha," Dela said, "why don't you take care of telling Mrs. Taylor? I'll be glad to talk to Evan. And, Ivy, you can inform your assistant about the meeting."

She was handing out orders like she was already the board president. I could feel my blood beginning to boil. Since I tend to turn beet red when I get upset, Amos knew I needed help. He linked his arm with mine and gave me a look meant to warn me to back down. Between Dewey's admonishment and the expression on Amos's face, I realized I was taking this situation too seriously. I was thinking about myself instead of what was best for the library. Sending a quick apology heavenward, I decided it was time to take the high road. Quite a few people had gathered around us, probably wanting to congratulate us on our appointments. This certainly wasn't the time or place for an emotional meltdown.

"I'll be happy to do that, Dela," came out of my mouth instead of the angry words I wanted to throw at her. I looked up at Amos. "Why don't we get to the dessert table before all of that wonderful lemon meringue pie is gone?"

He knew I was looking for a way of escape and quickly agreed, but before we could make our getaway, Dela grabbed my arm.

"Honey," she said loudly enough for everyone to hear, "I brought my measuring tape with me tonight so I could get some measurements at your house." She glanced around at all the people who stood nearby. "I'm Ivy's wedding planner, you know."

From the mumbled responses, nodding heads, and smiles sent my way, it seemed that most people were impressed. However, I thought I detected a few looks of abject pity.

I had to think fast. I had no intention of spending any more time that night with her. "I'm a little tired tonight, Dela," I said. "Why don't we do it tomorrow?"

She shook her head sorrowfully. "Oh, I can't do that, dear," she said. "I have plans tomorrow." She turned her head sideways and peered up at me with a look of amazement. "Now, Ivy," she said so everyone could hear her, "as I've already told you, I don't mind helping you with your wedding, but the least I expect is for you to work around *my* schedule. I don't think that's asking too much, do you?"

Before I could answer, Amos interrupted. "Dela, Ivy and I are going over to the bookstore after we leave here. Why don't you take Ivy's keys and go on to the house. If you finish before we get there, put the keys on the dining room table. That way we won't be there to interrupt you. I'm sure you don't need us interfering with your. . .your measurements."

I wanted to kiss Amos on the lips. Right there in front of everyone.

"That would be fine," she said. "It would be much better if I could work undisturbed." She held out her hand while I fished out a spare set of keys from my purse.

"What are you going to be measuring, Dela?" I asked.

"Oh, honey," she declared in her overly mushy, southern tones, "I have to find a way to get as many people as possible into your limited space. Of course, we'll have to move out some of the furniture. And then there are the decorations. I will need some wall space, so some of your little pictures will have to come down. Especially that huge, horrible tapestry in the dining room. It takes up too much space and the colors are just awful."

Amos tightened his grip on my arm. That "horrible tapestry" Dela referred to was my very favorite object in the house. It had been painted by Marion Biddle. It was a lovely picture of the back of the house and the lake during winter. Several children stood near the lake with their skates in their hands, while others skated on its frozen surface. I was one of those children. Marion had left it hanging in the house when they moved to Florida. "It needs to stay there, Ivy," she told me when I'd asked her about it. "That tapestry belongs to Winter Break." She knew how much I loved it, so I was thrilled when she told me it was mine.

"I'm sure we can remove it for the reception," Amos said quickly. "That won't be a problem." He shot me another look meant to keep me quiet. "Let's go, Ivy. We really need to get to the bookstore."

Before Amos pushed me out the door, I remembered Ina Mae. I looked quickly through the crowd that was focused on Dela and her halftime show. Near the coffeepot, I saw J.D. standing next to his wife. Since she wouldn't need a ride after all, I made my exit, grabbing my jacket from the small coatroom by the door.

I'd hoped I was free of Dela, but unfortunately she followed us out the door. "Don't worry about anything, honey," she called.

Since she was parked right next to Amos's patrol car, there was no way I could get away without responding. "Thanks, Dela," I said with a smile. It took almost everything I had to answer her in a civil way. Dewey's face and his comment about Bitty were the only things keeping me from throwing a real fit.

"That woman has some nerve," I said forcefully when we got inside the car. "If I want that tapestry up during our reception, it will stay up! How in the world does she think she can tell me what—"

"I told you this was a bad idea," Amos snapped, interrupting me. "But you wouldn't listen. Whatever happens now is on your head."

This was exactly what I'd been dreading, an "I told you so" from Amos. I sat in sullen silence while he drove us to the bookstore. Unfortunately, I had to face the truth. Maybe I had every *right* to be upset, but that didn't make my reaction acceptable. Aunt Bitty's voice resonated in my heart. "Anyone can love people who are easy to get along with, Ivy. It's loving difficult people in spite of their faults that gives us the chance to walk in God's love." I'd really had the best intentions for allowing Dela to be involved in my wedding, but I realized that unless I could adjust my attitude, this situation was going to turn into a big mess.

Once inside the store, with a fire going in the fireplace and Amos and me together on the couch in the sitting room, I felt the need to confess. "I let my emotions get away with me, Amos," I said. "I'm sorry. You're mad at me, Dewey's mad at me." The tears I'd managed to push away at the church made a return entrance. "I told Dela she could plan our wedding, so now I have to try to work with her and not be so touchy. And I'm sure she and Bertha will have some good ideas about the library."

Amos opened his arms and I cuddled up against him.

"I'm proud of you," he said softly. "You know, Ivy, I love a lot of things about you, but one thing I really respect is your ability to face your faults. It's a wonderful quality."

I wiped my face with the back of my sleeve. I needed a tissue, but I didn't want to leave Amos's embrace. "I know. You've told me that more than once." I ended my comment with a hiccup.

Amos chuckled. Then he pulled a handkerchief out of his pocket and handed it to me. "Maybe you need to hear it again. It might remind you that you're not a complete failure as a human being." He squeezed me and kissed the top of my head. "I love that you're so honest with yourself—and with me. It's one of the reasons I trust you."

I could have pointed out that I wouldn't have to use my so-called wonderful quality as often if I just quit goofing up so much, but I decided to stop while I was ahead. I wiped my face and spent the next couple of hours cuddled up with the man I loved. Finally, since it was getting late, we reluctantly untangled ourselves, and Amos drove me home.

As we pulled into my long, curving driveway, I noticed that Dela's car was parked in front of the garage. I'd almost missed it in the dark. At least she wasn't blocking the drive. "For crying out loud," I said. "She's still here? What in the world could take this long?" I grabbed Amos's arm. "Let's drive around a little longer, okay?"

Amos laughed. "No way. I have to get up early in the morning and so do you. This is a test of that new attitude of yours. Go in there and make nice, okay?"

I sighed. Great, another test. I was getting a little

tired of them. "Okay, okay." I turned my face toward his for a good-night kiss and then got out of the car. I steeled myself for what lay ahead.

I waved at Amos as his patrol car pulled away. Then I climbed up the steps to my front door. I was surprised to find it locked. When I stepped inside the house, I called out, "Dela?" When I didn't get a response, I called for her again. My house was strangely silent. I walked through the living room and checked out the kitchen. No Dela. A quick walk down the hall only revealed Miss Skiffins, my small, calico cat, napping in the spare room. I even checked the patio even though no one in their right mind would be out there as cold as it was outside. I yelled upstairs. Nothing. Would she have gone up there? Surely not. I climbed the stairs, calling her name, but all the rooms were empty. Confused, I went downstairs and stepped back outside. Her car was still parked in the driveway. I flipped on the yard light and thought I saw someone in the front seat. Why would Dela just sit there and ignore me? I felt a flash of frustration. This was Delaphine Shackleford. Common sense wasn't one of her virtues. I stomped down the stairs and marched over to her car. No reaction. Trying to push back my growing irritation, I tapped lightly on the driver's side window. She still refused to look at me. Finally, I opened the car door.

Dela's limp body fell sideways, hanging out the door. Her eyes were wide open and staring at me. And one of those stupid chopsticks was stuck beneath her ribcage.

I heard someone screaming, but it took several seconds before I realized it was me.

4

And what time did you say you left the church?"

"For the fifth or sixth time, Sheriff, it was around eight o'clock. I didn't check my watch."

Sheriff Milt Hitchens was a large man with a florid face and fingers the size of plump sausages. However, most of his bulk seemed to be muscle. I knew Amos took him seriously, and I would imagine that any criminal would think twice about crossing him.

"I'm sorry to keep goin' over this, Miss Towers," he said in a low, gravelly voice, "but it's very important we get all the details straight."

I wished Amos was here. He'd gone with another deputy to tell Barney Shackleford that his wife had been murdered. The pictures Dela had shown me of her dumb Chinese wedding kept flashing through my mind. I couldn't keep my eyes from tearing up. Strange how they seemed so ridiculous when I'd first seen them, and now. . . Okay, they were still ridiculous, but there was something endearing about a man who would dress up like that for the woman he loved. Barney didn't deserve the news he would receive tonight.

The sheriff and I were sitting in my living room while various law enforcement personnel availed themselves of my phone and, it seemed, the contents of my refrigerator. I didn't really care. Amos had told them to help themselves.

"Excuse me, Sheriff, may I talk to you a minute?"

A rather nondescript man in a dark suit interrupted us. I was getting used to it. It had been happening all evening. According to Amos, when there is a murder in a small, rural town like Winter Break, the sheriff's department and the Kansas Bureau of Investigation work the case together. This guy was most likely KBI. They all looked the same. Suits and serious expressions.

After speaking quietly for several minutes, Sheriff Hitchens came back and sat down next to me again. "Sorry for the interruption, Miss Towers. You said that the only thing you touched was the car door?"

"Yes, the car door." I blew my breath out through clenched teeth. I could feel the pressure building inside me. Dela was dead. In my driveway. My home had been invaded by law enforcement officers, and my fiancé's boss was treating me like a suspect. What more could go wrong?

"Miss Towers, I want you to think about that question very carefully. We will be fingerprintin' you so that we can eliminate your prints from any others on Mrs. Shackleford's car." He shook his head, his jowls bouncing like a nervous basset hound. "Sometimes people will try to pull out a knife or move a gun without thinkin'. You're certain you didn't do anything like that?"

I glared at him. "I've told you over and over the

only thing I touched was the car door. I didn't touch Dela because it was obvious she was dead. And I'm not brain dead. I would never have. . ." A sudden, sickening memory popped into my mind. To say that my whole body felt numb was an understatement. I looked at the sheriff in horror. "I—I—I, uh. . ."

He raised one eyebrow at me. "I take it you have somethin' to say to me, Miss Towers?"

I nodded dumbly.

"Would you like to actually tell me what it is, or would you like me to guess?"

I shook my head. "I—I—I mean, I think I may have touched the chopstick."

The sheriff's already ruddy face darkened several shades. "What do you mean, you *think* you may have touched the murder weapon?"

I wanted to protest that "chopstick" sounded better than "murder weapon," but it didn't seem to be appropriate. "Dela, that is, Mrs. Shackleford, was showing the chopsticks to me this afternoon in my bookstore. I. . .I picked them up. My. . .my fingerprints might still be. . ." I couldn't finish my sentence. The sheriff was looking at me the same way I imagine a hawk might stare at a mouse. I felt like dinner. "Sheriff, I assure you I did not kill Dela Shackleford. I wasn't anywhere near my house. I was with Amos Parker all evening. He can vouch for me." I wished I could get the squeaky tone out of my voice.

"I'll need you to come to my office tomorrow

morning, Miss Towers. You can have Deputy Parker drive you if you'd feel safer. The roads are still pretty bad."

All I could do was nod. In my mind, I was trying to see things from the sheriff's point of view. Dela was dead in my driveway. My fingerprints were on her car door *and* on the murder weapon. Nope. This didn't look good. As I watched the activity around me, I remembered that I had no motive. Sheriff Hitchens would see that. Besides, Amos was my alibi, and he worked for the sheriff. The convulsing butterflies in my stomach began to settle down a little. Perhaps murder might be a temptation *after* a Delaphine Shackleford wedding, but before? It didn't make sense.

As Hitchens walked away, I thought about pointing out my obvious innocence to him, but before I had a chance, Amos walked in the front door. I was so glad to see him I could barely contain myself, and I promptly forgot all about building a case for my exoneration.

I jumped up and hurried over to him. His expression was grim. I was certain telling Barney the bad news had been tough. "Are you okay?" I asked.

"Not really," he said, his brownish amber eyes narrow and his jaw tight. "This whole thing is unbelievable."

"How's Barney?"

Amos shook his head slowly. "He didn't take it well, Ivy. Not well at all."

Before he could tell me more, one of the other deputies called his name. He walked away and joined a group of several deputies and a couple of KBI agents.

They began talking to each other in low voices. Finally, Amos came back.

"Where is Miss Skiffins?" he asked. "With the front door opening and closing so many times. . ."

"Don't worry. I put her in the upstairs bedroom." I moved closer to him. "Someone followed me upstairs when I locked her up, Amos," I whispered. "It was like they thought I was up to something. What's going on?"

He sighed. "That's just the way it is. The KBI is tough on crime scenes. They keep us on our toes. Everything is important. Everyone is a suspect. When they first got here they were upset because we came in the house."

"What? But it's obvious she was killed in her car. Why would they want to check inside the house?"

"They're just being careful, Ivy. They need to make certain Dela wasn't attacked in here first." He shook his head. "I'm the one who told the guys they could come in and get something to eat."

"I'm sorry. Are you in any trouble?"

"No. The crime scene investigators concluded that Delaphine was definitely killed in her car. They think she'd been dead a couple of hours when you found her. Doesn't look like she ever made it into the house. She was stabbed once. The chopstick was pushed up under her ribs and hit her heart. She never had a chance."

I turned around and went back to the couch. I was starting to feel light-headed. The night's events, the realization that my fingerprints were on the chopstick that killed Dela, and the fact that it was after two o'clock in the morning and I was ready to drop combined to make me feel slightly woozy.

Then as suddenly as they had come, sheriff deputies, KBI agents, and some other people I'd never been able to identify began moving toward my front door like rats leaving a sinking ship.

"What's going on?"

"Wait here," he said firmly, "I'll be right back."

He joined behind the strange exodus. In a matter of seconds, my house was quiet again. Except for some empty pop cans and plates with the remains of cold cuts and chips littering my kitchen, everything was back to normal. It was as if a bad dream had come to an end. Unfortunately, I was pretty sure it would be waiting for me in the morning.

After a few minutes, Amos came back, closing the door behind him. "The coroner has taken Dela away, and her car has been towed to the sheriff's impound lot." He went into the kitchen and started cleaning up. I wanted to tell him to forget it, but I was too tired and too heartsick to say anything. When my kitchen finally had some semblance of order, he came over and sat down next to me. Without saying a word, he opened his arms and I melted into him. Now, the tears I'd been holding onto came without inhibition. Amos let me bawl for a while. When my sobs finally turned to sniffles, he handed me a paper towel he'd wisely carried with him from the kitchen. I wiped off my face and straightened up.

"Amos, the sheriff thinks I killed Dela."

"The sheriff does *not* think you killed Dela, but he has no choice but to follow up on every piece of evidence. Your fingerprints are on the car door and she was killed in your driveway. He can't ignore that. It doesn't mean he thinks you're a suspect."

"But what about that stupid chopstick? Aren't you worried about that?"

The calm expression Amos had been exhibiting for my benefit crumpled. "What about the chopstick?" he said slowly.

He hadn't heard. "My fingerprints are probably on it. Dela handed them to me today at the bookstore and I—I held them."

"You touched the murder weapon?" The size of his pupils and the lack of color in his face told me I was in trouble.

"Yes, Amos," I said sharply. "Although now I wonder why it didn't occur to me that just a few hours later, someone would drive one of those chopsticks into Dela's chest. What in the world was I thinking?"

Amos leaned over and put his head in his hands. After a few seconds he straightened up. "Everything will be okay. You were with me. He'll believe that."

I jumped to my feet. "He'll *believe that*? It sounds like you're trying to concoct an alibi! I *was* with you." I went to the refrigerator and grabbed a cold can of root beer. My throat was as dry as parchment. "You and I went straight from the church to the bookstore. Of course, I could have run out when you went upstairs to the bathroom. Let's see, you were gone what? Three or four minutes? Plenty of time for me to hurry outside, jump in my car, drive to my house, confront Dela in her car, and kill her with a chopstick from her wedding!" I waved my root beer can around like a conductor's wand. "That's it, ladies and gentlemen! Ivy Towers murdered the victim so she wouldn't have to walk down the aisle in a go-go dress!"

Amos raised his eyebrows and stared at me. "You're really overreacting, you know. And why would you get married in a go-go dress?"

I sat down on one of the stools at the kitchen breakfast bar and sighed. "Never mind. I'm being ridiculous. Here I'm worrying about myself, and I should be thinking about poor Barney."

Amos stood up and stretched. It had been a long night. I glanced at the clock. Correction. Long night and even longer morning.

"He was devastated," Amos said. "We asked him if he had any idea who might have attacked her. He didn't have a clue. As far as he knew, everyone loved her."

I shook my head. "I guess love really is blind. Dela ruffled a lot of feathers with her highbrow ideas and snotty attitude, but I can't think of a single person who would actually want her dead. In her own way, I think she really wanted to make our wedding special."

Amos came over and grabbed my hands. "We could get married in the grocery store with you holding a stalk of celery for your bouquet, and it would be special. I don't care about all the trappings. I just want to be your husband." My husband-to-be leaned over and kissed me. For the first time since I'd found Dela slumped in her car, I felt better.

"If you're planning to drive me to the sheriff's office in the morning, you need to go home." I looked at the clock on the kitchen wall. "We're not going to get much sleep."

"You go on upstairs," Amos said. "I'm going to stay down here."

I shook my head. "I can't let you do that. It doesn't look right."

His eyes narrowed and he put his hands on his hips. I knew what that meant. This wasn't going to be easy. "Ivy, someone was killed right outside your door. Most likely, the target was Dela, but I can't be sure. You cannot stay in this house by yourself until I'm sure it's safe. Right now I'm not the least bit concerned about 'how it looks.' I'll stretch out on the couch. Tomorrow we'll find someone else to come and stay with you."

I started to protest, but he pressed his fingers against my lips. "This is not open for debate. You get to bed, set your alarm, and wake me up at seven. We'll get some breakfast at Ruby's and then we'll drive to Hugoton."

I was too tired to argue, so I headed upstairs, released Miss Skiffins from her temporary prison, and fell into bed with her tucked under my arm.

I dreamed I was being chased by a large, ugly, papier-mâché dragon.

Ruby's Redbird Café was bustling. Pictures of Winter Break families, past and present, hung on the whitewashed walls, and the aroma of coffee and bacon permeated the air. Even though it was only a little after seven, almost every seat was taken. Most of Ruby's customers were farmers. Snow-covered fields didn't bring a halt to their heavy responsibilities. Farm animals had to be fed and tended to. Wood needed to be chopped to keep the fireplace going, and important repairs to equipment and buildings that hadn't been done during a busy crop season had to be addressed before spring.

Along with the farmers, other Winter Break residents gathered together because they liked to start the day with their neighbors. Quite a bit of gossip flowed through Ruby's every morning. Today was no exception. Diners leaned across the plastic red-checked tablecloths deep in conversation. The topic, of course, was Dela Shackleford. As soon as I walked through the door, I was surrounded by people asking for details. Ruby had rescued me by pushing through the crowd and hollering at everyone to "mind your own business or hit the road." Although a few nosy souls might have been willing to tempt her, in the end, no one was willing to miss out on one of Ruby's famous breakfasts. They were revered in Winter Break. No one could turn out a spread quite like Ruby—except Bert. He had already acquired his mother's talent for a perfectly formed omelet, and his blueberry pancakes were a crowd favorite. Together, Bert and Ruby ran the café with the skill of a highly trained drill team. Bert had added something new to Ruby's experience. His years as a fry cook in Texas had birthed a new language between him and his mother. It was something to behold. "A cuppa joe" was easy enough. But I had to ask Bert what "a pair of drawers" meant. Turned out to be two cups of coffee. For those who chose to pick up their food and take it home, Ruby would holler out the order followed by "and it's going for a walk!"

Although Ruby was still loud, thankfully she'd toned down some. Hard of hearing, she'd resisted a hearing aid for years. When Bert came home, he insisted she see a doctor. Now she sported a hearing device that lowered her screeching several decibels. Having Ruby sneak up behind you and yell so loudly your dinner ended up in your lap had been an everyday occurrence at the Redbird Café. Now at least her customers had a fighting chance.

"What'cha havin'?" Bonnie Peavey, the only waitress at the Redbird Café, leaned over the booth and smiled at Amos and me. Her dark eyes matched her ebony hair, which had been twisted into a braided bun. A little makeup brought out her flawless complexion. The change in Bonnie in a few months' time was remarkable. A year ago Bonnie had been a washed-out wisp of a woman, someone who seemed to blend into the background. Along with Ruby, she had been transformed by Bert's return.

We gave her our orders and told her that Dewey would also be joining us.

"I'll watch for him," she said, "but he always gets the same thing when he comes in for breakfast on Saturdays. Plain English muffin, poached eggs, a bowl of melon, and a cup of coffee."

I grinned at her. "Good for him. He's staying on track."

"We keep a close eye on him." She raised one eyebrow and looked around the room. "Boy, the place is sure buzzing. Someone said you found poor Mrs. Shackleford's body. You okay?"

I noticed that Newton and Marybelle Widdle, who were sitting at a table near our booth, leaned toward us, obviously hoping to hear something new about the dreadful murder. Since Marybelle was Bertha's best friend, I knew that whatever I said would be carried faster than the speed of light to my seeming archenemy.

I scooted closer to Bonnie and lowered my voice. "Yes, she was in my driveway. It was just awful."

"I'm sorry, honey," Bonnie said. She also noticed Marybelle and Newton's interest. "You need something, folks?" she asked loudly.

Marybelle and Newton flashed their most innocent

expressions and went back to their breakfasts.

"Do they have any idea who did it?" Bonnie asked. "The whole town is on edge. People who never lock their doors are installing deadbolts."

"It's never a bad idea to be safe," Amos told her, "but the killer is probably someone who knew Dela and was only targeting her. I don't think you have anything to worry about."

Bonnie nodded, but she didn't look convinced. Someone stepped up behind her, carrying a couple of plates.

"Well, now I know why my food is piling up in the back." Bert grinned at us and then handed steaming plates of eggs, bacon, and pancakes to the booth in back of ours. After checking to make sure his customers had everything they needed, he turned his attention back to us.

"It's probably because nobody wants your cruddy old food," Bonnie said, her dark eyes flashing with humor.

Bert sighed loudly. "See what I put up with? A true artist is never appreciated in his own time."

Amos laughed. "I feel exactly the same way," he said, looking at me.

"You poor things," I said, winking at Bonnie. "You're definitely legends in your own minds."

Bert chuckled, put his arm around Bonnie, and kissed her on the cheek. His salt-and-pepper hair framed an intelligent face with gray-blue eyes. He and

Bonnie made an attractive couple. I wondered if we'd be getting some news one of these days. Maybe there would be more than one wedding in Winter Break before spring came.

After a couple of minutes of small talk, Bert grabbed our order from Bonnie, waved a quick good-bye, and headed toward the kitchen. I heard him yell at Ruby, "Fry two, let the sun shine with two little piggies in the alley!" That was Amos's order of two eggs sunny-side up and a side order of sausage. I was getting pretty good at interpreting "diner speak."

Ruby's Redbird Café had always had a family feel to it, but now that Bert was here, there was a new energy. I saw Ruby walk out of the kitchen and step up to the cash register by the door. Maybe Bert had persuaded her to get a hearing aid, but he hadn't changed Ruby's outward appearance. She still sported a big Marilyn Monroe-styled wig. It was white blond, and it looked ludicrous on her ancient, wrinkled face. Ruby, like so many other women who'd spent time working outside on farms when they were young, had leather-like skin with deep cracks that ran down her cheeks. She usually wore no makeup except a slash of bright red lipstick that always caked up into the corners of her mouth by the lunch rush. Although her outward appearance was rather odd, folks were drawn immediately to her bright blue eyes, which sparkled with personality. To be honest, I was a little relieved that Bert hadn't been able to update his mother's look. I liked Ruby just the way she was. Brash, caustic, eccentric, and uniquely Ruby.

Amos was saying something about wishing he'd ordered pancakes instead of toast, when I saw Dewey walk in the front door. I waved to him and he began to thread his way through the crowded restaurant to our table.

"Boy, things sure are quieter when we have breakfast at the bookstore," he said as he slid into the other side of the booth across from Amos and me. "Even Saturday mornings aren't usually this bad." He nodded at Amos. "Good morning, son."

"Sorry, Dewey," I said, "but Amos and I have to drive to Hugoton this morning. I thought it would be better to grab a bite here so we could get away early. I'm beginning to wonder if that was a good idea."

Dewey reached over and took hold of my hand. "I could hardly believe it when you called and told me about Delaphine. How are you doing?"

It was the second time this morning someone had asked me if I was all right. I patted Dewey's hand. "I'm fine. Thanks for asking. This situation sure makes my temper tantrum from last night seem ridiculous."

Dewey peered at me from under his thick silver eyebrows. "I shouldn't have gotten on to you like that, Ivy. I'm sorry. To be honest, I was getting so much pressure from people wanting to be on the board, I was just happy to be done with it."

I waved my hand at him. "No. You were right. Aunt

Bitty would have accepted everyone selected as being picked by God Himself. She used to always say. . ."

"'God has a plan, and He doesn't always check with me before He formulates it,'" Dewey quoted.

I grinned at him. "I see Bitty's still talking in your head the way she does in mine."

Amos chuckled. "I'll find myself about to do something, and I swear I can hear her asking me, 'Have you spent any knee time on that decision, Amos?' " He shook his head. "I've had to back up and take another look at quite a few of my bright ideas."

Bonnie sidled up next to our booth. "Good morning there, Dewey," she said, patting him on the back. "The usual?"

Dewey crossed his arms across his chest and gazed up at the ceiling. "No, ma'am," he said in a deep voice. "I believe I'll start out with a sausage and cheese omelet. And use cheddar cheese on that. Four links of Ruby's homemade spicy sausage. And a side of blueberry pancakes. Lots of butter and syrup. Oh, and don't forget to bring an extra order of those wonderful hash browns. I like mine extra-crispy around the edges." He sighed with contentment and gazed at Bonnie with a twinkle in his eye.

"You bet. Right away. Poached eggs, melon, and a dry English muffin coming right up."

Dewey's pleased expression turned into a scowl. "My goodness, woman," he grumbled. "You sure know how to take the fun out of a meal."

Bonnie leaned over and kissed him on the head while Amos and I snickered. "We're just trying to take care of you, you crotchety old geezer."

"Bonnie," I said, interrupting Dewey's mumbling about too many people telling him what to do, "can we pay you ahead of time for our ticket? Amos and I have to get to the sheriff's office in Hugoton, and I want to get out of here as soon as we eat."

Bonnie came over to our side of the booth and leaned closer to me. "Sure. That's no problem. Let me total it and I'll bring it back. You can just pay me at the table."

I thanked her, but she stayed where she was. Obviously there was something else she wanted to say.

"I hope this doesn't offend you, Ivy," she said quietly. "I overheard someone say that the sheriff suspected you of killing Dela. Some folks said you had words with her last night at the city council meeting. Are you really under suspicion?"

I was startled to hear someone actually verbalize it. The idea had been floating around in my mind, but while it was locked inside my head, it seemed much more harmless.

"She's not actually a suspect, Bonnie," Amos said, coming to my defense. "The sheriff has to start ruling out people. Since Dela was killed in Ivy's driveway, she's got to be eliminated."

I was glad he hadn't mentioned that my fingerprints were also on the murder weapon. That was a story I didn't want circulating around town.

Bonnie looked around and leaned in even closer. "Listen, I don't like to repeat things I hear, but this place is a hotbed of gossip." She glanced at the Widdles, but they were deep in conversation. "I've heard more than one person say that Delaphine Shackleford was fooling around. You know, with someone besides her husband. I've been wondering if it might be important."

"It just might," Amos interjected. "Do you have any idea who it was?"

She shook her head. "Not a clue, Amos. If I'd wanted to find out, I probably could have, but as I said, I don't cotton to gossip."

"If you do hear anything more," Amos said, "will you let me know?"

Bonnie straightened up. "You bet. I have a feeling the stories are going to be flying like bees in heat. Poor Dela will be skewered six ways to Sunday before this thing is all said and done." With that, she turned and hurried off to put in Dewey's order.

"I can't believe the sheriff suspects you," Dewey blustered. His face was red with indignation. "While he's wasting taxpayer money bothering you, the real murderer could be halfway to Timbuktu by now."

"It's like Amos said, Dewey. He has to question everyone who's connected in any way, no matter how slight. He'll clear me soon. Please calm down. It's not good for you to get so upset."

"Well, I just never heard of anything so ridiculous."

At that moment it wasn't Dewey's diabetes that concerned me. It was his blood pressure. I reached over and stroked his arm. "Don't worry. Everything will be fine. I promise." My reassurances seemed to do the trick. Dewey's color began to return to normal. Feeling that he would be all right, I turned my attention to Amos. "What do you think about that? If Dela really was having an affair, the sheriff should know, shouldn't he?"

"Of course," Amos said solemnly. "If there's proof. Then we'd have to figure out what it means."

"It means that her boyfriend is a suspect," I said. "And so is Barney. Look, Amos, we need to be very careful about spreading rumors. Maybe I can poke around a little and find out something."

"I think you need to keep out of this," Dewey said gruffly. "If you don't stop sticking your nose in other people's business, you might get it chopped off one of these days."

"Dewey Tater," I said louder than I meant to, "I do not stick my nose in other people's business. Somehow I just seem to tumble into it. Besides, when someone is killed in my driveway, and I'm suspected, it becomes *my* business!"

"About that pretty nose of yours," Amos said. "You still need to find someone to stay with you for a few days, at least until we have a better idea as to why Dela was killed. How about calling your mom and asking her to come a little early? She and your dad plan to be here in a couple of weeks anyway."

I sighed. "It's not like they can take vacation whenever they want to, you know. They're running a mission. I don't know if she can just up and leave because her grownup daughter has gotten herself into another mess."

"I understand, but maybe she can come now and your dad can run things by himself for a little while. Someone needs to stay with you, and I can't think of anyone else. Emily's taking care of a baby, and according to you, I can't spend another night in our house without a chaperone."

"Why can't I move in for a while?" Dewey said. "At least until Margie gets here. Living in that small apartment over the store can get downright boring. A change of scenery would be nice."

Amos slapped the top of our table. "I think that would be a great idea. You could ride into work together each morning. What do you think, Ivy?"

I smiled at the both of them. "I can't think of anyone I'd rather have as a roommate. Let's do it. And I'll call my mom tonight. I guess it doesn't hurt to ask." Of course, I actually could think of someone else I would rather have living in my house, but I'd have to wait a few more weeks for that.

Bonnie showed up with our food, so further conversation was suspended for a while. I tried to concentrate on my breakfast, but the idea of Dela having an affair made my stomach feel queasy. All I could see was Barney's funny, happy face, standing at the altar in that ludicrous tuxedo. His wife was gone—his marriage ended. Was he getting ready to receive another terrible shock? A betrayal that Dela would never have a chance to repair? Or could it be that Barney wasn't the person he seemed to be? Could he have killed his wife with a chopstick from their wedding? I began to wish I'd never seen those goofy pictures, but for some reason, they made me feel very protective toward Dela and her memory. While Dewey and Amos chatted about something else, I sent a prayer heavenward, asking for help to uncover the truth about the murder of Dela Shackleford.

I thought you said you knew this was standard procedure, Ivy."

Amos's attempts to make me feel more relaxed weren't working. Even though I'd done my best to calm Dewey's concerns about the sheriff's interest in me, there simply wasn't any way I could reconcile the concept of being fingerprinted with anything other than criminal behavior. "Will there be a mug shot?" I asked Amos, using what he referred to as my "whiney voice." Newspaper reports with matching pictures paraded through my head. Celebrities who held little resemblance to their Hollywood glamour shots, staring at the camera with that stunned deer in the headlights expression on their faces. Would I look just as ridiculous?

"Of course not. You're not being charged with a crime. For crying out loud, Ivy. Quit letting your imagination run away with you."

"I'm trying not to, but we're driving to the sheriff's office in a patrol car, and I'm going to be fingerprinted like a common criminal. It's hard not to feel like I'm on the wrong side of the law."

Amos drew a deep breath and blew it out slowly. "Okay, you believe whatever you want to. When you get this way, there's nothing I can do about it."

He directed his attention to the highway. Conditions were beginning to get treacherous. A snowstorm had moved into the area. Most of western Kansas was getting a nice winter blanket of white, but since Winter Break already had about six inches on the ground, we were now up to about nine inches. Our windshield wipers beat a steady rhythm, trying to push away big, fat snowflakes that blew against our field of vision. It reminded me of the day I first came back to Winter Break to bury Aunt Bitty and decide what was going to happen to her beloved bookstore. I drove into town at night, snow almost blinding me, my own windshield wipers barely able to keep up. My intention was to get things squared away and get back to my life in Wichita. Yet here I was, a little over a year later, running the bookstore, engaged to the man of my dreams, and feeling as if I'd finally found the path God had prepared for me. It occurred to me that even in these strange circumstances, God's plan hadn't changed. This turn of events wasn't a surprise to Him, nor was it too much for Him to handle. "God doesn't ask us to walk by what we see and think, Ivy," Bitty used to say. "He tells us to walk by faith. What does faith tell you?" What I could see and feel was telling me that things didn't look good, but my faith told me that God had everything under control. It was my job to lean on His promises and trust Him to carry me through whatever came my way. I made the decision to go with the voice of faith, and as I did, a sense of peace settled over me and pushed away the self-pity that had seemed so strong only moments before. I scooted closer to Amos and hooked my arm around his. "I'm sorry. You're right. The most important thing is that we find out who killed Dela. I've only been thinking about myself."

The tightness in Amos's jaw relaxed, and he smiled at me. "I guess I'm a little tense, too. I'm sorry. You're the last person in the world who would ever hurt anyone. My deputy sheriff side seems to be in conflict with my fiancé side."

I squeezed his arm. "As someone who loves both your sides, I suggest you call a truce. Everything will be okay." I meant what I said, but as we pulled into a parking space in front of the sheriff's office, I felt a twinge of alarm. I made a conscious effort to reject it.

"Hello, Parker. Miss Towers." The sheriff's deep voice greeted us as we stepped inside the small office. Sheriff Hitchens stood next to a desk belonging to Marge McCarty. Nicknamed "Big Marge" because of her size, she didn't help to foster an atmosphere of friendliness to visitors who happened to wander into the sheriff's office. Of course, most guests didn't cross the doorway of their own volition. Unfortunately, I was one of those.

"Good morning, Sheriff. Hello, Marge." I flashed them both a smile I hoped was the very expression of total and complete innocence.

Sheriff Hitchens didn't seem moved, and Big Marge glowered at me. But that was par for the course with Marge. I reassured myself with the knowledge that she looked the same way at everyone.

"Someone from the KBI was supposed to be here this morning and interview you, but I guess a little snow was too much for him. Probably didn't want to mess up his cute little suit. So I guess it's just me. Lucky you. This way, please." We followed the sheriff to a room in the back where he quickly rolled some ink from a pad over a glass plate. He placed each of my fingers on the plate and moved them back and forth, getting the best possible coverage. After that, he placed them against several cards and handed me a damp towel when he was finished. It only took a few minutes, and it wasn't as bad as I had imagined. Then he put on plastic gloves, grabbed a long cotton swab, and motioned for me to open my mouth. He ran the swab over the inside of my cheek rather vigorously then dropped it into a plastic bag which he labeled and put in a metal container.

"That's all there is to it, Miss Towers," he said when he was finished. "Not as bad as you thought, was it?"

I shook my head. "No. Thank you, Sheriff."

He walked over and pulled the door closed, cutting us off from Big Marge and the outside world. "Sit down, please." He pointed to an old upholstered chair that had seen better days. I took a seat, trying to avoid the big rip in the fake leather. Amos came up next to me and put his arm on the back of the chair, resting it on my shoulders.

"When you saw Mrs. Shackleford Tuesday night at

the town meeting, was she wearin' the same clothes she had on that morning?"

"Yes, she was."

He reached for an envelope lying on a desk behind him. He pulled out some papers and handed one to me. "This is a list of everything we found on her. I'd like you to look it over. Tell me if anything is missin'—or if there's somethin' on the list that you *didn't* notice that morning." He looked back and forth between Amos and me. "Coffee?"

Although it was a nice gesture, it sounded more like an order the way he said it. We both nodded, even though I really didn't want any.

When he left the room I whispered to Amos, "What is he looking for on this list?"

"Anything different," Amos replied in a low voice. "Something that changed. It could point to motive. Especially if there's an item missing."

I looked the list over and was shocked to see that it even listed Dela's underwear. Her clothing, her purse and its contents, along with her jewelry, were also cataloged. "Her attaché case isn't here, but she probably took it home before going to the church." I started to put the sheet of paper back on the desk, but Amos grabbed my arm.

"Look it over again, Ivy," he said sternly. "I know it seems like a waste of time, but if you see anything, anything at all, it could really help."

I sighed and glanced over the record again. First I

read through the contents of her purse: *Makeup case, pocketbook with credit cards, driver's license, twenty-seven dollars in cash, two lipsticks, set of keys, aspirin, three writing pens, small notebook, breath mints.* Then I started on the other list of belongings: *red velvet skirt, red velvet matching jacket, black boots, gold and green ring with matching earrings and necklace, diamond and white gold wedding set. . .* The sound of the door opening behind me drew my attention away from the macabre list.

"How's it comin', Miss Towers?" The sheriff's booming tone made me jump, even though I knew he'd come back. He had the kind of voice that demanded attention.

"The only thing I don't see is her attaché case, Sheriff. But I imagine she took it home before the meeting that night."

Hitchens handed Amos and me each a cup of coffee in a Styrofoam cup. "What was inside the case?"

I briefly explained my discussion that morning with Dela, including the pictures of different wedding scenarios.

"Could there have been anything else inside that case?"

"I—I don't think so," I said, trying to remember. "I believe it only held pictures and ideas for weddings. Of course, I can't be completely sure."

"And she kept the chopsticks in her purse?"

"No. Originally they were also in the case. She put them in her purse after she had a hard time closing the clasp of the box they were in."

The sheriff leaned against the side of the desk and stared at me. "Is there anything else you can tell me?"

I glanced over the list once more. When I got to Dela's jewelry, I suddenly remembered something. "Her bracelet." I looked up at the sheriff. "Her bracelet's not here. The only reason I even recall it was because it seemed too big for her. At one point, it almost slid off her hand."

Hitchens took a small notepad out of his pocket and started writing in it. "Describe the bracelet, please."

"It was quite beautiful. Silver with clear rhinestones and. . ." I tried to bring a picture of the bracelet back to my mind. "Blue stones on the sides. I don't know, Sheriff, I didn't stare at it. I just noticed that it didn't seem to fit her."

Hitchens wrote a few more things in his notebook. Then he put it down and reached out for the list I still held in my lap. I handed it to him.

"Thank you, Miss Towers. That's quite helpful. Since she probably went home before the evenin' meetin' at the church, we'll check with her husband to see if she actually did drop off her case and her bracelet. Of course, if we can't find them, it would indicate that they were stolen."

I choked back a laugh. Sheriff Hitchens didn't look like someone who would find anything about a murder case particularly funny. "I really can't see that, Sheriff. The wedding pictures wouldn't be a good motive for murder, and the bracelet was obviously costume jewelry." I wanted to add that perhaps it would be prudent to track down all the humiliated bridesmaids from the go-go wedding and Dela's nuptials, but again, I doubted Hitchens would see the humor in my suggestion.

The sheriff slid the list of Dela's belongings back into the folder. "Are you a jewelry expert, Miss Towers?"

"No, but if Dela's bracelet was the real thing, it would have been worth a great deal of money. I doubt that she would be wearing it during the day. I also think she would have had it shortened to fit her. She wouldn't want to lose something that valuable."

Sheriff Hitchens raised his eyebrows and gave me a slow grin. "Quite an interesting observation. I've heard about you, Miss Towers. How you fancy yourself to be some kind of amateur detective." His smile disappeared and was replaced with something close to a snarl. "Let me make this perfectly clear. This isn't one of those silly novels where somebody who thinks they're Sherlock Holmes, Junior, outsmarts actual law enforcement personnel. I advise you to stay on your side of the fence and let me do my job. If you get in my way, even one time, I'll fix up a cell for you, and you'll sit out the whole investigation as a guest of the county. Do I make myself clear?"

I felt blood race to my face. I wanted to defend myself. Finding my aunt's killer and uncovering a murder that had happened many years ago in Winter Break hadn't happened because I was trying to be an "amateur detective." The suggestion was not only untrue, but it made it seem as if each situation was nothing more than some kind of trivial fishing expedition. And they were anything but that. I started to say something when Amos squeezed my shoulder.

"Is there anything else, Sheriff?" His words were carefully measured. I knew he was close to losing his temper, and I couldn't let it happen. Amos loved his job almost as much as he loved me.

Hitchens cleared his throat. "As a matter of fact, there is. First of all, I want you both to keep the missin' case and bracelet to yourselves. Until I find out if they were taken from the car, I don't want this information punted around by the bumpkins that hang around Ruby's Café. Secondly, I think you need to know, Miss Towers, that we received a call around eight thirty this morning from someone claiming that you killed Delaphine Shackleford."

I know my mouth dropped open, and I felt Amos's grip tighten on my shoulder. This wasn't good. I gently pried his fingers off before he caused me permanent damage.

"Before you get all hot and bothered, it wasn't anything I'd begin to take seriously." Sheriff Hitchens stood up and walked over to the door. "The woman believes you killed Mrs. Shackleford because you didn't want her on some library board." He seemed amused by our reactions. "I don't honestly think you killed her over some silly, small town appointment. But I think you need to know that you may have an enemy out there. Deputy Parker will tell you that we always get a few nutcases who call in tips when there's a murder. We learn to spot the phonies from the real thing." He swung the door open and waved at us to leave. As Amos walked past him, the sheriff grabbed his arm. "I want you to keep an eye on things in Winter Break, Deputy. It will be a few days before we start getting much information from the coroner's office or the KBI boys. I want you to poke around and see if you can find someone who had a real reason for wantin' Mrs. Shackleford dead." He fastened his narrowed eyes on me. "And I expect you to use *your* training skills. I don't want to hear that your girlfriend here is stickin' her nose in where it doesn't belong."

This was the second time in one day my nose was the topic of conversation. I was getting tired of it. "Thank you, Sheriff," I said as sweetly as I could. "I'm sure Amos won't need my help. He's quite capable of doing his job."

Hitchens opened his mouth to reply but was cut off by Big Marge, who was holding the phone next to her ear. "Sheriff, there's another one," she said loudly. "This time it's in Morgan City."

Hitchens swore under his breath and grabbed his coat. "You come with me," he barked at Amos.

"You better call Dewey and ask him to come and

get you." Amos hugged me and ran out the door, right on the heels of the sheriff. It was like some kind of instant evacuation. I didn't even have time to say good-bye. I could hear the tires of the sheriff's patrol car squeal as he pulled out of his parking space.

I turned around to find Big Marge staring at me. Well, this was going to be fun. I opened my mouth to ask if I could use the phone, but she pointed at a desk in the corner where another phone sat. While she began contacting other deputies and ordering them to Morgan City, I called Dewey. I glanced at my watch. It was only a little after ten o'clock in the morning, but I felt like I'd been at the sheriff's office all day.

As I sat near the front window, waiting for Dewey under the watchful eye of Big Marge, I kept wondering who in the world would suspect me of killing Dela. Was it someone who knew me? Someone who really believed I was capable of such a heinous crime because I wanted to be president of the library board? The idea was ridiculous. Still, it was disconcerting to be accused of murder.

I forced my thoughts back to Dela. Then I remembered Bonnie's comment about Dela having a boyfriend. I'd meant to bring it up to the sheriff. Now, I was glad I hadn't. I'd let Amos do it. I needed to heed the two warnings I'd already received and leave the investigation to him. Besides, I had a wedding to plan. I tried to mentally picture my wedding *To Do* list, but my thoughts kept wandering to that phone call. Did someone in Winter Break actually believe I was a murderer? Who could have made that phone call? And why?

Due to the snowstorm, Dewey and I didn't get back to Winter Break until after one o'clock. He dropped me off at the bookstore and went across the street to the Food-a-Rama. Because of the weather, we decided to have dinner at Ruby's then head to church without going home first. The road that led to my house could be tricky in the snow. I knew Amos would be glad to drive us back after the service. His patrol car was equipped with special tires that kept him out of ditches when the roads were icy or snow packed. My car, on the other hand, didn't seem to have any capacity for traction. Amos had pulled me out of so many snowbanks we'd pretty much abandoned using my car in the winter.

I sat down at my desk, looked up the number of the mission in China, and phoned my mother even though I knew it was very early in Hong Kong. I figured that if I'd ever had a good reason for waking up my parents, being suspected of murder was probably it.

After a few false starts, she finally figured out who I was. I tried to make the situation sound better than it was, but it didn't work.

"Another murder?" My mother's tone generally got higher the more upset she was. At that moment, I was pretty sure there were some operatic sopranos out there who would be jealous of her amazing reach. "What is going on out there? What is Winter Break, the murder capital of the world?"

As I assured her that we were still a long way from that distinction, I could hear my father speaking in the background. He's the calming influence in our family. Gradually, my mother's voice drifted down into normal ranges.

"I'll try to book a flight out this afternoon. But I probably won't get into Wichita until late tomorrow evening. Can Amos come to Wichita to pick me up?" Wichita was the closest large airport. It was possible to get a commuter plane to one of the smaller cities nearer to us, but they were horribly expensive.

"We'll figure something out, Mom. Just call me back at the house and let me know your flight information and exactly when you'll get in."

"Now, Ivy. That's *if* I can get a flight out today. I'll do my best."

"I hope this isn't going to cause you too much trouble." I had to wonder if dragging my mother away from her missions work was the right thing to do. Was I being selfish?

"Nonsense," she said. "We were coming in a few weeks anyway for the wedding. I've even talked to your father about arriving early so I could help. I'll be thrilled to see you and Amos." A male voice drifted through the receiver. "Just a minute, Ivy. Your father wants to say hello."

"Hi, *gong zhu*! I just wanted to say *wo ai ni*!" My father's deep Santa Claus laugh burst through the receiver.

Although in Mandarin *princess* didn't sound quite so delicate, gong zhu was my dad's new nickname for me. My previous moniker had been *bao bei*, which meant "precious." When he'd graduated to *wo de xin gan bao bei*, I'd been forced to ask him to find something else since it actually translated into "my precious." I was pretty sure even nasty hobbitses would find the phrase rather spine-tingling. Of course, my parents hadn't seen a movie for years, so when I tried to explain the reasoning behind my request, I ended up sounding slightly insane.

"Hello, *Ba ba*. I love you, too."

"I understand your mother is coming a little early. Wish I could join her, but I have a few things to wrap up here."

"That's okay. I'll just be happy to see you."

I said good-bye to my father and then my mother got back on the phone to reassure me that she would let me know her flight arrangements as soon as she could. After we hung up, I realized how much I missed them. My relationship with my mother had certainly improved since I'd moved to Winter Break. She had been horrified when I made the decision to make my home here and run my aunt's bookstore. Life in a small town wasn't my mother's cup of tea. But we'd finally come to an understanding and now, next to Amos, she was my best friend.

"Everything okay?" Isaac stood next to my desk, a look of concern on his face.

"Yes. My mother's coming to stay with me. She should get into Wichita sometime tomorrow night." I sighed. "I'm a little concerned about how we're going to get her here. With Amos spending so much time on these bank robberies, I'm not sure he'll be able to get the time off to pick her up. My car is useless in this kind of weather, and she won't want to rent a car. She doesn't like to drive in the snow."

His wizened face crinkled into a frown. "I wish I could help. I'm so useless in situations like these."

Isaac didn't drive. It really wasn't necessary in Winter Break, but that wasn't why he didn't own a car. He'd given up driving years ago, after being involved in a fatal accident.

"Don't worry," I said. "We'll figure out something."

He pulled a chair up next to my desk. "This rash of bank robberies seems so strange, doesn't it? I would think someone who wanted to acquire a large sum of money would target one of the larger financial institutions."

I sighed and leaned back in my chair. A look out the window told me it was snowing even harder. "Amos said the same thing. I think it's one of the reasons they're having such a hard time finding this guy. In a way, hitting smaller banks is pretty smart. They're easier to rob, but you're right, I don't imagine they keep much money readily available."

The front door of the bookstore flew open, helped along by a hefty gust of wind. Amos stepped inside. He stomped his boots on the entry mat and pulled off his gloves. "Boy, it sure feels nice and warm in here. It's awful out there."

After hanging up his coat and removing his boots, he came over and parked himself on the edge of my desk.

"So what happened?" I asked. "Isaac and I were just talking about the bank robberies."

He rubbed his hands together to warm them. "It's the strangest thing I've ever seen. It appears to be one man. Somehow, he knows just when to hit the banks."

"What do you mean?" Isaac asked. "Is one time better than another?"

"Yep. Usually in small towns, there's not much cash in the till. Except on certain occasions. Like the bank in Mollyville. The only real money that comes in is after a big weekend at the Mollyville Hotel Restaurant. You know, that big tourist attraction on Highway 54?"

We both nodded. Converted from a hotel built in the 1800s, the Mollyville Hotel drew people from all over Kansas—and other states. They only served one thing: family styled fried chicken dinners with all the fixings. It was always busy, and those who didn't make reservations generally didn't have much luck getting in.

"So this guy strikes after someone brings in a large deposit?" I asked.

Amos took off his hat and smoothed his honey-blond hair. "That's what's happened every time. In Chevron he struck the Savings and Loan right after the county fair."

"But that would mean he knows the local routines," Isaac said. "So it would appear that he is someone known by the residents."

Amos nodded. "That's exactly what it means." The frustration in his voice was evident. "But how could one guy know so much about so many different towns? We've checked with all kinds of people. No one has any idea who it could be."

"What about people who don't belong?" I asked. "Someone new in the area?"

"We've tried that, too. No one has reported anyone suspicious." He chuckled. "Except in Brinkman. There was a story about a strange man hanging around the bank the day before the robbery. Turned out to be a sign painter from Liberal. The bank was updating the lettering on the front door. He wasn't too happy about being suspected of bank robbery."

"Surely the banks in Stevens County are taking better precautions now," Isaac said.

"We've been doing everything possible to get them to implement necessary safety measures. So far only one of them even had a security camera. And it wasn't working. I'm not sure what's going on in other counties where this guy's been, but my guess is they're doing the same things we are to try to prevent another robbery."

"I haven't heard any reports of violence," Isaac said. "I guess that's a blessing."

"Unfortunately, that's not true," Amos said. "He shot a customer in Chevron who tried to stop him."

"Why, Amos," I said, "this is the first time I've heard that. It wasn't in the newspaper."

Amos shrugged. "The wound wasn't serious. The robber shot the guy in the leg, but he's fine. We're keeping that particular detail under wraps along with a few other things. In any investigation, it's important to have a few secrets. Helps us to make sure we've got the right person."

"But shouldn't people know he's armed?" I asked. "For their own protection?"

"The banks in Kansas know about it. But to be honest, I don't think he's dangerous. He's never tried to hurt anyone else. The man who was shot made a foolish move. Our robber friend fired in an attempt to stop him, not kill him."

"What about his getaway car?" I asked. "Has it been seen?"

Amos crossed his arms across his chest and stared at us. "Are you two thinking about joining the investigation?"

"Don't be silly," I snapped. "We're just interested. It's better than thinking about Dela's murder."

Amos sighed. "Well, you're right about that. And yes, his cars have been spotted almost every time."

"You said 'cars,' " Isaac said. "He drives more than one?"

"He steals someone's car, drives it to the bank, and robs it. Then he drops the car off somewhere and takes his own vehicle to make his getaway. Actually, it's pretty smart. Pinching a car in a small town is too easy. People leave their keys in the ignition. They think they're immune because they're not in the big city." He shook his finger at us. "And before you ask, there are no fingerprints, so he's obviously wearing gloves. Not too unusual in the winter. And we haven't found any usable tire tracks. Either the stolen car is found in a parking lot, or it's abandoned in a place where there's so many vehicles going in and out, we can't tell what he's driving. This morning we found the truck he used parked at a large twenty-four-hour bingo parlor outside of Morgan City. So many people had come and gone, we couldn't get any information on him or his car."

"Well, Deputy," Isaac said, "I don't envy you with this one."

"I have a hunch you won't be chasing this guy much longer," I said.

Amos frowned at me. "What do you mean?"

"He can't keep this up. He's attracting too much attention. My guess is he's trying to grab as much money as he can from these little banks because they're easier to hit. That's going to change, and he knows it. I'll bet you a jar of huckleberry jelly that his reign of terror will come to an end any day now."

"You might be right," Amos said thoughtfully. "Which means if we don't catch him soon, we may never bring him in. And that reminds me. Alma gave us four more jars of jelly. And I've got about ten more jars of Bubba Weber's honey."

"Bubba's going to have to find a place to store his honey," I said crossly. "First he fills up your house, now he's loading up my basement. Cecil built those shelves downstairs to house Marion's preserves, not Bubba Weber's honey."

Amos grinned. "Are you thinking about putting up your own preserves?"

"Even if I wanted to, I don't have the room. I'm too busy hoarding honey."

Amos shrugged. "You're right, but it won't be much longer. Dewey's cleared out one of his back storage rooms in the store. He's going to start keeping the honey there."

"Good. I like Bubba, but this has gone on too long."

"After we're married, we're going to have to do something with that basement. It needs to be updated, and we need to do something different with the laundry. Carrying clothes up and down the stairs is too much trouble."

I smiled at him. "I like my basement. It has character. And I don't mind carrying the laundry. It's good exercise."

"A lot of the older houses around here were equipped with dumbwaiters," Isaac interjected. "Besides the washing, basements were used to store fruits and vegetables. It was cooler down there and produce kept longer. It was a simple matter to send food or clothes up and down with the dumbwaiter."

"Unfortunately, my house doesn't seem to have one," I said. "But maybe my handsome, soon-to-be husband can design something himself."

Amos chuckled. "Or your handsome soon-to-be husband can find a place upstairs to move the washer and dryer. I don't like those stairs. They're too rickety. Besides, you've got to be tired of chasing Miss Skiffins out of the basement every time you open the door."

My small calico cat had developed an obsession for huckleberry jelly. I'd caught her on the kitchen counter more than once, licking the jelly off my toast or English muffin. She'd figured out there was jelly in the basement, but thankfully she hadn't figured out how to open the jars yet.

Isaac stood up and offered Amos his chair. "Well, this was a most stimulating discussion, but I need to go home and prepare for church." He smiled and looked a little embarrassed. "Alma and I will also be dining at Ruby's before this evening's service."

I wanted to tease him about Alma, but I'd found out the hard way that there were certain things Isaac took very seriously. And his relationship with Alma was one of them.

He excused himself and left through the sitting room. He lived right next door. In fact, his home was actually part of the bookstore. Aunt Bitty had turned part of the building into an apartment for her faithful employee and close friend.

Amos slumped down into the chair vacated by Isaac. "Let's quit talking about the bank robberies for a while, okay? I need a break. This whole thing is giving me a headache." He scooted the chair closer to me and reached for my hand. "Sorry about this morning. I respect Sheriff Hitchens, but sometimes he can be a real jerk."

"I'm okay. Don't worry about me. Are you going to check with Barney about Dela's attaché case and bracelet?"

He nodded. "Yeah, Hitchens asked me to follow up and let him know. I can't imagine the killing had anything to do with either one of them. Dela probably left the case at home because she didn't need it for the meeting, and if the bracelet was as loose as you say, maybe she took it off because she didn't want to lose it."

I stared at him for a moment. "Yeah, maybe."

"What's wrong? Is there something bothering you?"

"This sounds silly, Amos, but the more I think about it, the more I realize that the bracelet didn't belong."

Amos cocked his head to the side and looked at me quizzically. "What do you mean, 'it didn't belong'?"

"Dela was always so *coordinated.* Everything went together, you know. Fashion-wise, color-wise. But the bracelet didn't go with her outfit. It was too dressy and had blue stones set in silver. Her earrings, necklace, and ring all had red stones set in gold. Dela was always super coordinated. Her jewelry always matched her outfits and all the pieces matched each other."

Amos pursed his lips. "That's interesting." He stood up. "Why don't I pick you up around five for dinner? I think I'll run over to Barney's now. If the bracelet's not there. . ."

"It could mean something," I finished for him.

Amos learned over and kissed me on the nose. "Just for the record, I love your nose. You can stick it into my business whenever you want to."

I reached up and hugged him as hard as I could. "Thank you. Maybe I'll only stick it where it's wanted from now on."

"That might be a good idea, for a while at least."

I suddenly remembered my mother and asked him about picking her up tomorrow night.

"I don't think that will be a problem. Our robber keeps banker's hours. Let me know as soon as you have all the flight information."

After he left, I realized I had only a little over an hour before we left for Ruby's. I cleaned my desk and checked my email. I had several inquiries about books. Noel had sent me a message about some new editions he'd acquired for the library, including an entire set of Charles Dickens. I wanted to let Hope and Faith know, and I also wanted to see how the library was coming along, so I decided to have Amos pick me up there. It would also give me a chance to see Faith. We'd become really close over the summer. She'd been despondent over the death of her parents in an automobile accident, and I was someone who was willing to listen. Someone outside of her family. She was living with her aunt, Inez Baumgartner, Emily's mother. She had definitely made strides toward healing, and working in the library had given her something constructive to do.

I wrote a note on a sheet of paper telling Amos that I would be at the library and taped it to the front door. Thankfully, the glass storm door would keep it from getting soaked by blowing snow. It was a primitive way to communicate, but there wasn't any cell phone service in Winter Break. Unless another larger city sprang up near us, no cellular company was going to put up a tower for a town our size. At first, it was a major inconvenience. But now, it didn't bother me much at all. Except for times like this. I could call Amos's dispatcher, but unfortunately, that was Big Marge. I could have also called Barney, but I didn't want to disturb him quite yet.

Trekking two blocks in a blizzard isn't easy. One step forward is usually accompanied by two steps back, but I finally made it. I had to bang my fist on the library door since it was locked. Finally, Hope pulled up the shade on the window and peered out to see who was making so much racket.

"Ivy!" she said after pulling the door open. "Get in here before you freeze solid."

I gratefully stumbled inside. It took awhile to get my blood circulating again, but after stomping my feet a few times and rubbing my hands together, I felt confident enough to venture forward. I gazed around the room and was thrilled to see the progress that had been made.

"It looks great," I said as I took off my coat. "You two have really been working hard."

Hope grinned. Her short ash-blond hair and turned-up nose always made me think of a pixie I saw once in an illustrated book. Her small stature added to the picture in my head.

"I think we'll be ready to open right after Valentine's Day. You've brought us so many books it's taking us a long time to catalog everything." She laughed. "Isn't that wonderful?"

I was delighted by Hope's enthusiasm. When she first came to Winter Break, the grief of losing her grandmother was still very fresh. She was so quiet and introverted, I wondered sometimes if she would ever come out of her shell. But here she was, excited about the library and making new friends.

"Hi, Ivy!" Faith came around the corner of a long row of bookshelves. She was another person who had changed after coming to Winter Break. Strange how so many people had found redemption in this small town.

"Hello! I was just telling Hope how impressed I am by how far along the library has come. It sure looks better than it did the first time Dewey showed us this old building."

Hope held out her hand for my coat. I slid it off and handed it to her. She carefully laid it across the back of a nearby chair.

Faith laughed. "I was really excited about the library until we stepped inside the front door. Boy, I wasn't certain whether this place was a blessing or a curse!"

I shook my head. "After the feed store closed down, Dewey just locked the door and forgot about it. Too bad the mice didn't forget."

"And the birds who found their way in through the hole in the roof," Hope said. "But then so many people pitched in to clean it up and make repairs, it came back to life." She smiled and looked around. "I think it's just perfect now."

The building was still pretty old and it certainly wasn't what I'd call "perfect," but it definitely had charm. The exposed pipes that ran across the ceiling had been painted white, and some of the men from church had painted the walls a deep green, repaired the wooden floor, and built shelves that ran along the walls and down through the middle of the main room. Up near the front was a large desk for checkouts and a seating area set aside for library clients. We still needed some nice, comfy chairs for future bookworms. So far, we'd only collected a few beat-up folding chairs from the church basement.

The library reminded me only a little of the bookstore. It would never have quite the same relaxed ambience of Miss Bitty's, but it would still be a terrific resource for the residents of Winter Break. Although my interest was heading more and more toward collectible and rare volumes, I would always keep some special volumes to be read by residents who wanted to enjoy a cold winter afternoon next to a crackling fire or hide out from the rain and dream between the pages of a book. Bitty would have wanted it that way.

I handed Hope a list of the new books Noel was donating to us.

"Oh, my," she said softly. "A complete set of Dickens? And the Father Brown mysteries? How wonderful."

G. K. Chesterton was a favorite of mine. His character, Father Brown, had entertained me on many occasions. "And I'm working on completing our Agatha Christie selections." I smiled. "With all the Nancy Drew editions we already have, we're going to end up with a wonderful selection of mysteries." Hope and Faith both grinned at my comment. We were all mystery buffs.

"How about some coffee, Ivy?" Faith asked. "Inez gave us her extra coffeemaker so we could have something hot to drink while we're working. It does get a little cold in here when the wind blows hard."

Although I'd felt warm when I'd first come inside, now I could feel a definite draft around the windows. "I'd love some coffee. I'll also speak to Dewey about making this place a little more airtight. No one will want to stay very long if we can't keep the winter wind out."

I took my coat from the back of the chair where Hope had placed it and put it around my shoulders. Then I sat down in the chair. "If I'm in the way, just kick me out. Amos will be picking me up for dinner in a while."

"Don't be silly," Hope said. "We can visit while I finish cataloging this stack of books."

We spent some time talking about literature. Then the discussion turned to Dela's murder and my upcoming nuptials. I was beginning to see that both events were going to get tied together in people's minds since almost everyone knew that Dela had been my wedding planner. For the first time, I started to wonder if Amos and I shouldn't postpone our marriage for a couple of months. The danger was that we could find ourselves waiting until spring. Although Winter Break usually got more measurable snow than anyplace else in the state, waiting until April was taking a chance. I really wanted to be married in the snow—on Valentine's Day.

I'd just started telling Hope and Faith about my trouble finding a gown when someone pounded on the front door. I was closest to the door so I opened it to find Amos standing outside. As he stepped through the door, a blast of cold air pushed snow in after him.

"Sorry," he said, looking down at the clump of snow quickly melting on the small carpet in front of the door. "It's snowing like blue blazes out there—even for Winter Break."

"No problem," Hope said, jumping up from where she'd been sitting on the floor with a pile of books. "We've been cleaning it up all day." She grabbed a towel from the desk and tossed it down toward Amos's wet boots. "Just stomp on it some so it will soak up the water."

"How about a quick cup of coffee?" I asked him. "We still have plenty of time."

He grinned. "Sounds great. The heater in the patrol car is having a tough time against the wind. I'm frozen to the bone."

Faith poked her head around the corner of one of the bookshelves where she'd been working. "I'll get it. How do you take it, Amos?"

"Black is fine," he said. "Right now the only thing I care about is how hot it is."

"Excuse me for a few minutes, will you?" Hope said. "I'm missing a book. It's probably at the bottom of one of those boxes in the back room."

"If you need any help let me know," Amos said, scooping up the wet towel from the floor and handing it to me.

She thanked him and disappeared, leaving Amos and me alone. I laid the wet towel on top of some plastic sheeting in the corner.

"Did you talk to Barney?" I asked in a low voice.

Amos's gaze moved toward the spot where Hope had been standing. "Yes. Dela's satchel is there."

"What about the bracelet?"

Amos looked around once again. "He didn't know what I was talking about. He even showed me Dela's jewelry collection. It's huge, but I went through it carefully. There wasn't anything like what you described: a silver bracelet with clear rhinestones and blue stones on the sides."

"So it wasn't there?"

He shook his head. "That bracelet's gone, Ivy. Whoever killed Dela took it. All we have to do is find it and we've got our murderer."

The sound of shattering glass startled us. We turned around to find Faith staring at us, the coffee cup lying in pieces on the floor, and her face as white as the snow swirling around outside the window.

8

We checked to see if Faith had been burned by the coffee that splashed up against her jeans, but she was fine. It was obvious to Amos and me that her reaction was connected to our discussion, but Faith wouldn't admit it. She kept repeating that she'd simply lost her grip on the coffee cup. Her expression was grim and she was obviously distracted. Hope kept shooting me worried looks behind Faith's back, but all I could do was shrug at her. There was no way I could tell her what we'd been talking about since Sheriff Hitchens had warned us to keep our mouths shut about the bracelet.

Amos made some excuse about wanting to get to Ruby's before it got any later. I hugged Hope and Faith before I left. I could feel how tense Faith was under her sweatshirt. We'd spent so many long afternoons talking about her life and the death of her parents that knowing she was shutting me out hurt my feelings a little. I whispered in her ear, "If you need to talk to me about anything, all you have to do is call." The only response I got was an almost imperceptible nod.

Amos and I fought our way to the car. When we got inside, he started the engine and turned the heater up full blast. We were greeted with a burst of icy air.

"Well, what in the world was that?" I asked through chattering teeth.

"I don't know," Amos said in a grim voice. "But we were supposed to keep that little fact about the missing bracelet to ourselves. Good job."

"What do you mean, 'good job'? Seems to me you were the one shooting your mouth off in there. Besides, we didn't actually tell anyone. Faith overheard us." I turned toward him, pulling my coat around me as tightly as I could. "Amos, she knows something about that bracelet. It was obvious."

He stared out the car window at the library. "I'd like to think she just got rattled hearing us talk about the murder, but here's something I didn't get a chance to 'shoot my mouth off' about. I got a call from Hitchens as I was leaving Barney's. You know that call that came into the office claiming you'd killed Dela?"

"Yes, of course I remember. I can't get it out of my mind."

Amos turned toward me and lowered his voice as if someone might be hiding in the back seat, listening to our conversation. "It seems it was only the first of several so-called tips."

I felt my heart leap inside my chest. "You mean someone else has accused me of murder?"

"No. Not you."

"Not me? Then who?"

He removed one of his gloves and put his hand in front of the heater. "Let's see. One person called to confirm what Bonnie told us. That Dela was having an affair and Barney killed her. Someone else said that

Barney killed her because she was going to uncover some kind of insurance fraud he was involved in. And another advised the sheriff to look for a missing bracelet. That robbery was the motive."

"They knew about the bracelet? Amos, where are these calls coming from?"

"Unfortunately, from different places. Two of them were from the kind of cell phone you can buy at any discount store. We can't trace them. And the other one was from a pay phone in Hugoton."

I turned this new information over in my mind. "The tip about Dela having a boyfriend could be made up by anyone. And Barney being involved in some kind of fraud could be conjured up by someone who knows he works in insurance, but how many people would know about the bracelet?"

"I have no idea, but right now most of the tips point to Barney." Amos put his glove back on. "Look, we'll talk more about this later. Let's get to Ruby's before we freeze to death out here. I don't think I want to add to the wild speculation spinning around town. Some anonymous caller is liable to decide we committed suicide to hide our guilt over killing Dela."

I hit him on the arm. "Amos! Don't make a joke out of this. It isn't funny."

He rubbed his arm. "I didn't say it was funny. Quit beating me up." He put the car in gear and we slowly turned around in the snow-packed street and headed toward the restaurant.

"You can see why I'm concerned about Faith's reaction," he said through chattering teeth. "I need to know what's going on. Do you think you could talk to her? You guys are good friends."

I scooted up as close as I could to him, pointing the still cold air from the heater toward us. "I'll try, but ever since She's been helping at the library, we haven't spent much time together. All I can do is give it my best shot. I'm sure she had nothing to do with Dela's death."

"I don't think she did either, but we need to find out what she knows about the bracelet before she slips up and says something that could get her into trouble."

"Oh, Amos. Do you think she could be in danger?"

"Who knows? This whole situation is really confusing. I don't suppose you're ready to come up with one of your Sherlock Holmes moments and tell me who the murderer is?" His eyes crinkled with humor, but his expression certainly wasn't jovial.

"Don't let Sheriff Hitchens ever hear you say that. The truth is I can't even come up with a Watson moment." I saw Ruby's up ahead. It was already filling up and it was only around five thirty. Something I'd been trying to remember took that moment to pop into my head. "You know what this reminds me of?"

"I don't have a clue." He successfully steered us into a parking space. I thanked God once again for the great all-weather tires the county put on its patrol cars.

"A mystery I read once. I can't remember who wrote it."

"Great," Amos fumed. "The heater's finally starting to work." He put the car in park but kept the motor running. "What about it?"

"There was a murder. Then all kinds of people in the town started getting letters that accused them of different things. Adultery. Murder. Larceny. All kinds of disreputable happenings."

Amos looked amused. "Disreputable happenings, huh? How did it turn out?"

"The murderer was sending the letters. He did it to throw suspicion off himself. But the interesting thing was, he realized that he had to include himself among those who received a letter, because if he didn't, it could point to him as the author—and the murderer."

Amos turned off the engine and stared at me. "That's interesting, but how does that apply to our situation?"

"Who knows? What's normal in a situation like this? In a small town like Winter Break, everyone knows your business. Are there really that many people who think they have pertinent information about Dela's murder, or could all the calls be coming from one person?"

Amos stared at the snow piling up on the windshield. "We've gotten lots of tips before over all kinds of things, but I'd have to say that this is different. All of these calls are anonymous. That's not normal. I mean, why wouldn't people leave their names? Or just come into the office and talk to the sheriff if they thought they knew something important? Or even come to me? I don't relish telling Barney that someone accused him of killing his wife. Even mentioning that she may have been fooling around isn't something I look forward to. Especially now. Unless we find Dela's killer quickly, we'll have to follow up on these tips. We won't have any choice."

The tiny amount of warmth we'd been able to generate was rapidly disappearing. "Look, you haven't been around much lately," I said. "Maybe these people who are calling will come to you if they know you're available. Let's get inside Ruby's so the word will spread that you're in town. Besides, I'd like to lose this nice shade of blue I'm developing."

I put my hand on the door handle, but Amos reached over to stop me. "One more thing," he said. "I also tracked down the phone used by your anonymous caller." He pointed toward the payphone near the front door of Ruby's Café.

"That phone?" I asked incredulously. "It's clearly visible from inside Ruby's. Maybe someone saw who called."

"My thinking exactly. Let's talk to Ruby and Bonnie. See if they can remember seeing anyone using the phone this morning."

"What time did the sheriff say that call came in? We were having breakfast between seven and eight o'clock."

"The sheriff said the call came in around eight thirty."

"So whoever called waited until we left Ruby's. I wonder if they knew we were going to see the sheriff."

"Look," Amos said, "it won't do any good to guess who called. Let's see if anyone noticed someone on the phone around eight thirty." He released my arm and we got out of the car. The steps up to the restaurant hadn't been cleared so Amos held onto me so I wouldn't slip. Once we opened the front door to Ruby's, welcome heat washed over us. We threaded our way through the full tables and found a booth in the back. The table was still dirty, and Bonnie's tip was sitting there, but we didn't care. We were cold and hungry, and Ruby's was the place to be under those conditions.

We'd just sat down when Emily came up to the booth and slid in next to me. "Hey! I've been trying to call you all day. Where've you been?"

I shook my head. "If I told you, you wouldn't believe me." The last thing I wanted to do was to recount my time being fingerprinted at the sheriff's office. "Let's save that story for our next girls' gab fest, okay? What's going on?"

"I talked to Mama. Ivy, she's so thrilled about the dress. She can hardly wait to get started. She would like to meet with you and do a few measurements."

"Oh, great. My very favorite thing. Can't she just measure you and double it?"

Emily laughed. "No, because it would be too big, you silly woman." She stood up. "Just give me a call, and we'll set something up soon. I better get back to

Buddy. We're having a 'night out' together. I didn't want to take Charlie out in this weather, so Mama's watching him."

I saw Buddy sitting across the room with a big, sloppy grin on his face. I waved at him. "Looks like your hubby's pretty happy to have some time alone with his wife."

Emily smiled and gazed around the crowded restaurant. "If you call this having some time alone. But I guess we'll have to take what we can get."

I grabbed her arm before she could get away. "You and Buddy plan a real grown-up evening soon, okay? Go to Hugoton for dinner. Amos and I will watch Charlie."

Amos's eyebrows shot up so high they almost disappeared into his hair. "Whoa. What are you volunteering me for?"

I batted my eyes at him. "You need to get some practice, Amos. Someday we might hear the patter of little feet."

"Well, at least for a while, they better belong to Miss Skiffins," he said, shaking his head.

Emily and I both laughed, and she leaned over and hugged me. As she waded through the crowd toward Buddy, I couldn't help but notice how happy they looked. I could hardly wait until Amos and I were married. I was even more excited now since I wasn't too worried about all the planning that still needed to be done. My mother was a human tornado. I was confident she would whip everything together when she got here.

"Hey, you two." Ruby pulled the dirty dishes off our table and dumped them into a large plastic basket. Holding the basket under one arm, she wiped down our table with a wet rag. "How's it goin'?"

I could have said a variety of things, but instead I smiled and said, "Fine. How about you?"

Ruby gave us a look at her false teeth. "Couldn't be better. Seems like you and Amos ain't the only people gettin' hitched."

"Oh, Ruby! Bonnie and Bert?"

She nodded so hard I was afraid her wig was going to bounce off. "He asked, she said yes." She slapped her rag back inside the basket. "If you'd told me a year ago that I'd be announcin' Bert's weddin', I woulda called you a two-faced lyin' weasel." Her eyes got shiny. "But look at me now. And it's thanks to you two." She wiped her hand across her eyes. "Dinner's on me tonight, folks. And dessert, too. You better eat up, 'cause you know how stingy I usually am."

Amos chuckled. "Ruby, you're about the least stingy person I know. Thanks for the dinner. We'll gladly accept."

She started to leave but then turned around again and leaned over next to me. "I promise, honey, you're gonna have a weddin' feast like you never imagined. I'm pullin' out all the stops. And I'm givin' you somethin' for a weddin' gift that most of the people in this town would give their right arm for." She grinned widely and left, yelling at people in her way to "move it or lose it!"

Amos stared at me with his mouth open. "Wow, Ivy. Maybe she's going to give you the recipe."

That was really all he needed to say. "The recipe" could only be one thing. The secret formula for Ruby's Redbird Burgers. Down through the years, many people had tried to wheedle it out of Ruby through bribery, threats, and coercion. In fact, there had once been a town meeting called to figure out how to get Ruby to fork over her burger secrets before she kicked the bucket. So far, all avenues had led to defeat. The only person she'd ever told was my aunt Bitty. And Bitty wouldn't even tell me. "A promise is a promise, Ivy," she'd said. "If people can't trust our word, how can they believe us when we tell them they can take God at His?" She'd died with the secret of the Redbird Burger. Now, it seemed that I was to be given the greatest honor Ruby Bird could bestow. Maybe to some people it might seem silly, but to me it was one of the most touching gifts anyone had ever given me.

"Maybe you better not count your burgers before they're hatched," I told Amos. "She might mean she's passing along one of her wigs. How do you think I would look?"

He chuckled. "Not so good. Let's hope that never happens."

"What'cha havin?" Bonnie stood poised with her order pad, a big smile on her face.

"I hear congratulations are in order," I said. "I'm so thrilled, Bonnie."

She blushed. "Well, don't go telling a bunch of people about it. We're trying to keep it kinda quiet. We're thinking about a small ceremony."

"I think you should have whatever you want, Bonnie. But I imagine the whole town would turn out to see you two get married. It's a real love story." I choked up over the last few words. Two people loving each other for over thirty years, finally getting a chance to be together. It didn't get more romantic.

"Oh, for crying out loud," Amos said with a smirk. "You women and *romance.* Good thing we men are more practical."

Bonnie grinned. "Bert took me to the peach orchard where we buried that box of his trinkets so long ago before he left town. He gave me a new jewelry box full of all those old things. And right in the middle was a small velvet case with my ring in it. Then he got down on one knee and asked me to marry him." She sighed. "He might be a man, but he's as romantic as they come." She wrinkled her nose at Amos. "Besides, you're a big talker, but my guess is you're pretty romantic yourself."

Amos held his hands up. "I plead the fifth."

Bonnie laughed and lowered her voice to a whisper. "By the way, I tried to find out who poor Dela was fooling around with, but the only thing I could figure out was that it didn't happen here. It was back in Dodge City where she came from. Some relative of Marybelle Widdle's who lives there told her that they'd seen Dela out several times with some good-lookin' man. But no one I talked to has any idea who it was." She clucked her tongue. "If you want my opinion, it's just a nasty piece of gossip without anything to back it up. I'd forget about it."

"Thanks, Bonnie," Amos said. "I appreciate your help."

She scribbled something on her order pad. "Ruby said dinner's on the house tonight. Bert's got a new dish. This is the first time we've served it. I think you ought to give it a try."

"What is it?" Amos sounded a little suspicious. Change at Ruby's didn't come easily.

Bonnie looked a little embarrassed. "Veal Marsala with risotto and steamed asparagus."

Amos and I just stared at each other. Veal Marsala in Ruby's Redbird Café? It just didn't sound right.

"No one's ordering it," Bonnie said. "They're all afraid to try it."

I knew Amos had been looking forward to Ruby's famous Wednesday night meatloaf, but some things are more important than meatloaf. "Bring us two orders of Veal Marsala, Bonnie," I said as loudly as I could without looking totally deranged. "It sounds wonderful."

Amos looked like he wanted to say something, but he just offered Bonnie a weak smile and a nod.

"Thanks, folks," she said quietly.

When she walked away, Amos scowled at me. "Thanks for ordering for me. What if I hate Veal Marsala?"

"Have you ever had it?"

"No, but that's not the point. I—"

"Oh, hush up," I whispered. "You were going to order it anyway. We both know it."

We were getting stares from several of the tables around us. I noticed J.D. and Ina Mae Feldhammer sitting in a booth across the room. I waved at Ina Mae. She smiled and held up her hand. She hadn't been to the bookstore for about a week. I pretended to pick up a cup and drink from it and she nodded. J.D. didn't seem to notice. In fact, he was going over some paperwork and didn't appear to realize his wife was even there. I wondered if her marriage was the source of her sadness. She never talked about anything personal when she came to visit. We just shared recipes and talked about books we liked.

I noticed Bertha Pennypacker sitting with the Widdles. Bertha and Marybelle had their heads together, and they were looking at Amos and me. As usual, I seemed to be the topic of conversation. Newton just stared off into space, lost in his own thoughts.

When Bonnie came back with our coffee, I remembered to ask her about the phone call.

"This morning?" she said, wrinkling her nose. "Boy, we were so busy, I can't remember if I even looked out the window. I'll ask Ruby and Bert if they noticed anything and get back to you. Is it important?"

"It really is, Bonnie," Amos said in a low voice. "But please keep it to yourself, okay?"

"Sure thing," she said, leaning in close so no one around us could hear her. "I'll let you know what I find out. Maybe you better deputize me, Amos. I'm sure doing a lot of nosing around for you."

"I would if I could, Bonnie," he said with a grin. "You're better than some of the deputies I work with."

She laughed and walked back to the kitchen.

After she left, I started to ask Amos a little bit more about the phone calls that had come into the sheriff's office, but he hushed me. "I can't take the chance that someone will overhear us. We've already spilled the beans once today. Let's talk about it later when we're alone."

We spent the next few minutes talking about picking up my mom and what would happen if the snow got much deeper. I wasn't sure if I wanted to come back into town tomorrow to open the bookstore. I was pretty sure no one was going to want to wade through all the white stuff to read a book, and Isaac had finished his work for the week. I had just mentioned my concerns to Amos when Isaac and Alma came in. They looked so cute together, Isaac in his black topcoat that appeared to have been styled in the 50's and Alma dressed in a deep blue wool cloak with a matching knit hat. The table next to our booth was empty, so Isaac steered Alma our way.

"Hello," Alma said in her soft, demure voice. "How nice to see you both."

Isaac, ever the gentleman, came over and shook Amos's hand. "Good evening, Deputy." He turned and gave me a little bow. "And you, too, Miss Ivy."

"Hi there, Isaac. Getting a little dinner before church?" Amos asked.

Isaac helped Alma off with her coat and held out her chair. "Yes. It seemed the thing to do. Alma was going to cook for us, but I decided she needed a night out." He smiled and took off his own coat. "But I must tell you that she is a culinary master. I have thoroughly enjoyed all her meals." He patted his small stomach. "I might actually be putting on weight."

Isaac was a wisp of a man. Even a pound would help. As strong as the wind was sometimes in Winter Break, I was afraid he was going to be carried away one day.

Suddenly, the doors of the kitchen swung open. Bert Bird was bringing out two plates of steaming food. Bonnie followed behind with a bread basket. Either we were being treated to a very small parade or Amos and I were getting ready to be presented with our dinners. With all the flair he could manage, Bert deposited our plates in front of us.

"Veal Marsala," he said loudly. "I'm glad someone in Winter Break is willing to take a risk. *Bon appétit!*" Then he whirled away, leaving Amos and me the center of attention at Ruby's.

Bonnie set the bread basket down and turned to Isaac and Alma. "What'cha havin'?" she asked.

Isaac looked at me and smiled. Then he raised his eyebrows at Alma. "I believe we will have the Veal Marsala, too. It looks wonderful."

Bonnie winked at him and yelled to Bert, who was standing in front of the doors to the kitchen, watching us. "Two more Italian moo moos!" Bert flashed us a big grin and disappeared into the kitchen.

While Amos said a prayer over our food, I silently told God that I had no intention of being deceitful, but I was determined to say the Marsala was good, no matter what it tasted like. Amos and I speared a forkful of veal, mushrooms, and sauce and stuck it in our mouths at the same time. The explosion of garlic and butter sauce, along with the tender medallion of veal, was incredible. "Delicious!" I said. I had half a mind to stand up and give a review so everyone could get back to their own lives.

Amos nodded, smiled big, and took another bite. I think he was just trying to get out of saying anything, but the gusto he displayed seemed to work. Everyone went back to their conversations. In the next few minutes, I heard several people call Bonnie over and ask if it was too late to change their orders. The Veal Marsala was a hit, and Ruby's had a new favorite. I couldn't help wonder if Bert would still be here someday when Ruby was gone, cooking the old standbys but bringing some new taste treats to the town of Winter Break.

We ate quickly since it was getting late and we wanted to avoid the stampede to the church. I'd just finished my last bite when Bonnie came back to our booth. "I asked around about the people using the phone this morning," she said quietly. "Bubba Weber told me he used the phone after he dropped off our jars of honey. But he had to wait for Bertha Pennypacker to get off the phone. She seemed real secretive about whoever she was talking to. She told Bubba to wait inside until she was finished."

"Did you ask Bubba what time that was, Bonnie?" Amos asked.

She nodded. "He said it was right around eight thirty. He remembers because he needed to deliver some honey over to Marvin Baumgartner's place. He lives quite a way outside of town and Bubba wanted to make sure he and Edith were back from visiting her sister in Cawker City."

"Thanks, Bonnie," I said. "That's exactly what I needed to know."

She handed me a bag she was holding. "I heard about the dog. Thought you'd like to have some bones." She smiled and patted my shoulder. "You come by any time, and we'll give you some scraps. Poor thing needs to get inside where it's warm. Good luck."

I thanked her before she scurried back to the kitchen. Then I flashed Amos my most superior expression. "Who do you suppose could have told

Bonnie about the dog? It sure wasn't me."

Amos frowned at me. "You caught me, Nancy Drew. I think he's a lost cause, but I know you well enough to realize you're not going to give up. I'm afraid you may have to learn that some creatures never heal from abuse."

"But I truly believe that with God all things are possible, Amos. For that reason alone, I have to try. I've never found anything so broken that God couldn't mend it." For some reason my eyes wandered toward Bertha Pennypacker, who was glaring at me. I wondered what was really causing her to hate me so much. Was her anger coming from some past pain?

I looked at Amos. "I can hardly believe that Bertha despises me so much she would actually try to implicate me in a murder investigation."

"I'm sorry, Ivy," he said gently, "but you have to remember that Bertha's problems aren't your fault. For some reason, she's decided to focus her unhappiness on you. My guess is that she's jealous of you for some reason. You represent something she wants and doesn't think she has."

"I know that, but to actually accuse me of killing Dela. . ."

"Thankfully, it wasn't successful. I know what she did was wrong, but I think we need to put Bertha on the shelf for a while. We have other things to think about that are a little more important right now."

I agreed with him, but there was still a wound in

my soul. I'd never been disliked so fiercely before. And it hurt.

We joined the mass exodus of Ruby's patrons on their way to church. Amos stood in the street and directed some of the cars trying to back up and head for the church so we wouldn't end up with a huge pileup. By the time we drove into the church parking lot, there weren't many spaces left. He let me off near the entrance while he parked the car. When I stepped into the foyer, I almost ran into Ina Mae Feldhammer. She seemed to be waiting for someone.

"Hi, Ina Mae," I said, smiling. "How's your mother?"

The corners of her mouth turned up quickly then dropped as if they weren't used to going in that direction. "She's hanging in there," she said, her voice so faint I could barely hear her. "I think she's looking a little better."

"I'm so glad. Are you waiting for J.D.?"

"No. I was waiting for you." She looked up at me, her large, chocolate-brown eyes and her sad expression reminding me of the lost dog that was hanging around my house. "I was wondering if you were going to open the bookstore tomorrow. I mean with all the snow and everything. . ."

"I really hadn't made up my mind yet." I got the feeling that her question was more of a request than an inquiry. "Can I call you tomorrow and let you know?"

She nodded quickly and turned to leave.

"Where's J.D.?" I asked, not wanting her to leave yet.

"He has to see someone about a property."

"It's pretty bad weather for that, isn't it?" I asked.

She stared down at her shoes. "J.D. says the real estate business is a twenty-four-hour-a-day job." She shrugged. "He goes wherever he has to. Business comes first."

I wasn't so sure she accepted his priorities as easily as she said. The front door opened and Amos came in. I put my arm around Ina Mae. "Are you sitting by yourself tonight?"

She looked away from me and nodded.

"Why don't you sit with Amos and me?"

Again, a small smile twitched the corners of her lips. "That would be nice."

We entered into the sanctuary as the music began. While we sang, I prayed that God would show me how to help the small, timid woman. She certainly needed a friend.

After praise and worship, Pastor Taylor stepped up to the podium. I respected him as much as anyone I'd ever known. Not only was he a wonderful source of spiritual strength when it was needed, he truly lived what he preached. Winter Break residents knew if they needed anything, he would be there. When a fire destroyed part of the bookstore last year, Pastor Taylor and Bev were among the first people on the scene, helping to repair the damage and put Miss Bitty's Bygone Bookstore back together. Although God had used him to touch my heart on many occasions, one thing he'd said when I was a kid had always stuck with me. *The goodness of God gives me strength.* I trusted in that goodness—in every circumstance. I'd met people who believed God was a fiery judge, just waiting to punish them for their mistakes. But I'd learned that God loved me, accepted me warts and all, and *always* wanted the best for me. And Pastor Taylor was right. It gave me strength.

He looked out at the congregation, his expression solemn. "Before tonight's lesson, I want to pray for Barney Shackleford and his family. And I want to remind everyone that although we might not be related to Barney in a physical sense, we are related in the Spirit. Please reach out to our brother during this tragic time. Barney has expressed his wish to have Dela's service here in Winter Break, and he asked me to extend his personal invitation to all of you. There is no date set at this time. When I have more information, I will pass it along to you. Barney does have several relatives staying with him, so if you can deliver some food to them, I know they would appreciate it. Please contact my wife. She has a signup sheet for meals."

I was surprised that the funeral would be held here. I'd assumed it would be in Dodge City, and I couldn't help but wonder about the arrangements. Pastor Taylor led us in a beautiful prayer, thanking God for welcoming Dela into His kingdom and asking for peace and comfort for Barney and the families. Then he asked us to turn to the eighteenth chapter of John, where he read about Peter's denial of Christ at His crucifixion. After that, we turned to Matthew 10:33, where he read, "'But whoever disowns me before men, I will disown him before my Father in heaven.' " Pastor put down his Bible and looked out at us. "So by his own words, Peter deserved to be disowned. Rejected by Jesus in front of the Father. But what did Jesus do?" Then he read the story of the women who went to the tomb and found it empty. "They found an angel inside the tomb. Jesus was gone. What did the angel say?" Pastor Taylor smiled. "Remember that Christ had every right to turn His back on Peter. In the hour of His greatest need, the disciple who claimed to love Him denied he even knew Him. But notice that the angel says this: 'You are looking for Jesus the Nazarene, who was crucified. He has risen! He is not here. See the place where they laid him. But go, tell his disciples and Peter, "He is going ahead of you into Galilee. There you will see him, just as he told you." ' " Pastor Taylor closed his Bible. "Notice that Jesus singled out Peter. He wanted to make certain Peter knew He was coming to see him and that He still loved him and still considered him to be His friend. You see, God's love is eternal. There isn't anything you've ever done that will cause God to turn His back on you. We give up on ourselves sometimes, but God is always there, calling to us. He wants you to know that no failure is too much for Him. There is nothing you've ever done that could break your relationship with Him so badly that it can't be mended."

I remembered what I'd told Amos about the dog. It was similar to what Pastor Taylor had just said about our own bond with God. I heard an odd choking sound next to me. When I turned to look at Ina Mae, I saw that tears were streaming down her face. Not knowing quite what to do, I reached over and took her hand in mine. When she looked up at me, there was so much pain in her face, I wasn't sure what to say or do. But she squeezed my hand and hung on. We stayed like that throughout the rest of the service.

Pastor Taylor brought up many more examples from the Bible of God's unchanging love. When he was finished he asked if there was anyone in the congregation who'd felt estranged from God and needed to restore fellowship with Him. I felt Ina Mae's grip strengthen, but she stayed seated as several others went forward. Finally, I whispered in her ear, "If you want to go up front, I'll go with you." It was all she needed. Still holding my hand, she stood to her feet and we walked up together. When Pastor Taylor prayed for her, she cried harder, but when he was done, I saw the first real smile I'd ever seen on her face. By the time she let go of my hand, it was almost numb. I had to open and close it several times to get all the feeling back. After everyone had been prayed for, we went back to our seats and waited to be dismissed. When Pastor Taylor gave the final blessing, I asked Ina Mae if J.D. was going to pick her up. She shook her head. "I don't think so. He said he might be really late."

"Why don't you let me drive you home?" Amos said, overhearing our conversation.

"Thank you. That would be wonderful." Again, a smile lit up her face. As we stood to leave, I saw Faith standing next to Emily. She saw me, too, and turned her head.

"Amos, why don't you get the car?" He nodded and took off for the foyer. "Ina Mae, I need to talk to someone for just a minute. Can I meet you by the front door?"

She nodded. "I'd like to stop by the bathroom for a minute anyway. I must look a mess."

I grinned. "I've had raccoon eyes so many times in church, people think it's the way I wear my makeup."

She laughed. "I won't be long. I'll wait for you in the front."

We went our separate ways and I began searching for Faith. I found her standing next to the coatrack. I had the feeling she was hiding—from me. I grabbed her arm. "I want to talk to you. Let's go to the library."

I led her to the church library, which was unlocked. After pulling her inside, I locked the door to discourage anyone else from entering, and then I pointed to a pair of chairs with a table and a lamp between them. Faith plopped down into one of them but she didn't look very happy about it.

"Faith," I said as gently as I could, "I'm concerned about you. Today at the library—"

"I told you," she said, interrupting me, "I just lost my grip on the coffee cup. Why don't you believe me?"

I could almost see the petulant child I'd first met months ago when she first came to Winter Break. The change in her had started right here—in this library. Now here we were again. I shook my head. "Honey, we've shared almost everything there is to share. I thought you trusted me. What happened?"

Her eyes filled with tears. "Oh, Ivy. I don't know what to do. I know you care about me, but I don't want to get anyone in trouble."

"Faith," I said as gently as I could, "Dela Shackleford is dead. She had the right to finish her life. Someone took that away from her. When it comes to murder, there can't be any secrets. Don't you see that? If you know something that could lead to uncovering her murderer, it's your responsibility to tell someone. If you don't want to tell me, you can talk to Amos."

She hung her head. Her dark, straight hair hung down, covering her face. When she raised her head, tears were running down her cheeks. "What if I say something that makes someone look guilty who isn't? That's not right."

"That's not up to you to decide. We have laws and people whose job it is to uphold them. If this person isn't guilty, he or she won't be charged with anything. But you can't decide what's right and wrong. It's not your job."

I could see the torture in her face, and it disturbed me. "Honey, please trust me. Tell me why you reacted so strongly when Amos and I were talking about Dela's murder."

She didn't say anything for several seconds. Then she sat up straight and looked into my eyes. "That bracelet? The one Amos was describing?"

I nodded, encouraging her to continue.

She took a deep breath. "I saw it, Ivy. Hope has it."

With Ina Mae and Dewey secured in the backseat, Amos maneuvered his car carefully through the snow-covered streets to Ina Mae's house. As soon as the heavy snow was through falling, several Winter Break farmers would attach snow plows to their tractors and clear the roads. It was one of the side benefits of living in a farming community. Our downtown streets would probably be cleared by tomorrow afternoon. The only down side was that after being plowed, there was usually a sheet of ice left behind. Businesses would put down ice melt or salt to clear their own walks, but it was too expensive for the town to salt all the streets. Besides, salting might make a difference for a day or two, but then snow would surely move in again. In Winter Break, a superior sense of balance, along with a good pair of snow boots, weren't luxuries. They were necessities.

It was still snowing, but thankfully the wind had died down. Harsh, blowing flurries had changed to big, fluffy flakes drifting down from the sky, creating a beautiful winter dance that was highlighted by the glow of streetlamps. I would have enjoyed it more if Faith's words hadn't kept resonating in my mind. Why would Hope have the bracelet? I'd mulled over the problem pretty well by the time we reached the Feldhammer house.

Amos got out of the car and opened the door to the backseat, helping Ina Mae to step out.

"Thank you, Ivy," she said before she closed the car door. "You don't know how much tonight helped me. I'm so glad you were with me."

Although I didn't know what her battle was, I knew the feeling of reaching out to God and having Him reach back. I'd never forgotten the story of a young man who'd been brought up in another religion. He'd spent his life trying to get attention from the god he'd been taught to follow. Yet there was never any response, no matter what he did or how much he prayed. Then someone told him about Jesus. The first time the young man cried out to Him, God answered, showering him with His love and forgiveness. He was amazed to find a God who really listened; who really cared for him and was actually able to change his heart. The young man became a Christian and spent his life as a missionary in his own country. Seeing the expression on Ina Mae's face brought that wonderful story to my mind.

"Please come by for coffee when you can," I said. "I may not open the bookstore tomorrow, but I plan to be there Friday. I'll call you tomorrow and let you know for sure."

She nodded. "Thanks, Ivy. Goodnight, Dewey."

She smiled and shut the door. I watched her make her way up to the front door, Amos holding her arm so she wouldn't slip. *Nothing so broken that God can't mend it.* I'd seen this truth played out time and time again. *With God nothing is impossible.*

"Quite a night," Dewey said from the backseat. "I'm glad you were there for Ina Mae."

"Me, too," I said, twisting around to look at him. "I was just wondering why we try so hard to solve our own problems before we turn them over to God."

Dewey shook his head. "I guess it's because most of us haven't figured out how helpless we are without Him. We might be able to do all things through Him, but by ourselves we're pretty puny."

I chuckled. "Isn't that the truth?"

The driver's side door swung open and Amos climbed inside. I wanted to tell him about the bracelet, but Sheriff Hitchens's admonition kept me from saying anything in front of Dewey. I waited until Amos pulled up in my driveway and got the car as close to the front door as possible.

"Dewey, do you mind going on in?" I asked, handing him the keys. "I'd like to talk to Amos for a minute."

Dewey grinned. "You two aren't gonna sit out here and neck, are you?"

"Now that you mention it, I think that sounds like a pretty good idea," Amos said innocently.

I slugged him on the arm. "Oh, hush up. It's too cold to 'neck.' Our lips would freeze together."

Dewey opened the car door in the back. "I don't know, Amos. That doesn't sound too bad. Maybe you should give it a try."

"Shut the door and get in the house, old man," I said, laughing. "I'll deal with you later." We watched Dewey walk up the steps. He had a small satchel with him. I assumed his pajamas were inside. "I just realized," I said with a sigh, "Dewey's my babysitter."

"Don't be silly," Amos said. "Now, what's up?"

I told him about Faith and the bracelet.

Amos sat back in his seat and let out a low whistle when I finished. "Hope Hartwell has the bracelet?" He thought for a moment and then shook his head. "Why in the world would she kill Dela for some cheap bracelet?" He turned to stare at me. "You know, you said you got a pretty good look at that thing. Are you sure it was rhinestones? Could it have been diamonds?"

I held up my hands in mock surrender. "How would I know, Amos? The only diamond I've ever had is the one in my engagement ring. I assumed it was costume jewelry because no one in their right mind would wear something that expensive unless they were at some kind of formal dinner. And trust me, the meeting I had with Dela yesterday morning wasn't that fancy."

"Okay, settle down. I'm just trying to figure this out. The truth is we can't be sure the bracelet Faith saw is actually Dela's. Maybe she saw a bracelet that was similar."

"You've got a point, but it would certainly be an odd coincidence. Two identical bracelets showing up at the same time?"

"Did Faith say it had blue stones like the other one?"

"Yes, she described exactly what I saw, Amos. I really think it's Dela's."

Amos grunted. I could almost hear the gears turning in his head. "The point is, whoever took the bracelet removed it from Dela's body for one of two reasons. Either it was valuable, or somehow it would tie them to the murder."

"That makes sense," I said, "but I have a hard time seeing Hope as a cold-blooded killer. Usually I get a pretty good sense about people."

Amos snorted. "You're great with piecing clues together, but you've spent time around two different murderers and your 'spidey sense' never kicked in one time. I think we better stick to the facts."

I stuck my tongue out at him. "Okay, maybe you're right. But I still can't imagine Hope driving a chopstick through Dela Shackleford's heart because of a bracelet. She seems like such a nice person."

"The truth is we don't really know Hope. She hasn't been in Winter Break very long. We certainly can't rule her out because she 'seems like a nice person.' "

With the car idling, I could feel the cold creeping in again. I tried wrapping my arms around my body to generate some warmth. It wasn't working.

"So now what? Do we talk to Hope? Or just turn this information over to the sheriff?"

"*We* don't do anything," Amos said. "Sheriff Hitchens

asked *me* to investigate this murder. I should tell him about Hope, but I haven't actually seen the bracelet. I don't know if I can just take Faith's word for it." He put his arm up on the back of the seat and rubbed my shoulder. "I don't suppose you told Faith not to mention to Hope that she talked to you?"

"Yes, I did, smarty-pants. I'm not completely brain dead."

"Good job. And don't call me smarty-pants." He leaned over and kissed me. And our lips didn't stick together. "You get inside. Make sure all the doors are locked. When you hear something from your mother, let me know."

"I will." I kissed him again. "Call me in the morning, okay?"

"You got it. If anything unusual happens tonight, you call me right away. Promise me."

I reached over and touched his cheek. "I promise, but the only unusual thing I'm likely to hear is Dewey's snoring. No one is after me, Amos. Please stop worrying."

He shook his head. "I'm not worrying. I'm just trying to be wise. You're the most important person in my life. I want to make sure you stay safe."

"I understand," I said with a smile. "I feel the same way about you." I kissed him once more, then I turned to open the car door.

"Hey, wait a minute," Amos said. "I've got Bubba's honey and those jars of huckleberry jelly in the trunk.

We need to get them inside before they freeze."

I waited while he retrieved a large box from the trunk. When we got to the front door, I started to open it and then I stopped. "Amos, where are my keys?"

He frowned. "I think your brain's frozen. You gave them to Dewey. Now open the door. This box is heavy."

"No, I gave Dewey my regular set of keys. I'm talking about the spare keys I gave to Dela at the church. I just realized that I never got them back. And the list of Dela's belongings at the sheriff's office only listed one set of keys. She had to have her own set. She was driving her car. Where are mine?"

"I looked at that list, too. You're right. There was only one set of keys." He stared at me with a worried expression. "I don't like not knowing where those keys are. I'll check with the sheriff. Maybe they just forgot to document both sets." He shifted the weight of the box in his arms. "Right now, though, I'd appreciate it if you'd just open the door. Unless you want a front porch littered with broken jars of honey and huckleberry jelly."

"Sorry." I pushed on the door and found it unlocked. After directing Amos to put the box on the kitchen counter, I hugged him while Dewey watched us.

"I'll let you know what I find out," he said when he let me go. He looked at Dewey. "Keep an eye on our girl, Dewey. I'm counting on you."

When he left, I stood at the front door and watched him pull out of the driveway, his brake lights disappearing behind a curtain of snow. I glanced around once before closing the door, but I didn't see the dog. I said a silent prayer, asking God to keep him safe. I also asked for help finding my keys. I didn't want to panic. There was probably a good explanation for their disappearance, but knowing that the last person who had them was a victim of murder made me nervous.

Once inside, I finally started thawing out. Dewey and I drank hot chocolate and sat in front of the fireplace in the living room while Miss Skiffins curled up next to me and slept. We talked for a while about the bookstore. I was just telling him about my attempts to acquire a first edition of *Little Women* by Louisa May Alcott, when there was a knock on the front door.

Dewey got to his feet. "You expecting anyone?" he asked.

I shook my head and checked my watch. It was a little after ten o'clock. "Nope."

He went to the front door and looked through the peephole. "Well, I'll be," he said. "It's J.D." Dewey swung the door open. Sure enough, J.D. Feldhammer stood on the porch.

"Goodness gracious, J.D.," I said when he stepped inside. "What are you doing out in this kind of weather?"

"I'm really sorry to bother you folks," he said. "But my car slid off the road. I'm stuck in the ditch just a little ways down from the entrance to your driveway."

Dewey closed the door behind J.D., and I jumped up and went over to where he stood, shivering. "Here, give me your coat. Let's get you warmed up."

J.D. smiled and handed me his all-weather coat. Then he took off his black rubber snow boots and set them on the mat. "Sure glad you're living out here, Ivy. The nearest farm is Bubba Weber's and that's about another mile up the road."

J.D. took off his gloves and his knit cap. I took those, too. "Let's lay these out near the fire," I said. "See if we can dry them out some."

He followed Dewey and me into the living room. "Maybe I can get Odie to come and pull me out. He's got that big truck."

"I'm sure he'd be more than happy to help," I said, "but let's call Amos first. He's always pulling people out of the snow. He's got chains in his trunk. I'll bet he can have you back on the road in a jiffy."

J.D. looked relieved. "Well, if you don't think it would be too much trouble. . ."

"Not at all. You sit down in front of the fire and warm up. I'll call Amos and get you a cup of hot chocolate."

"Thanks, Ivy. I really appreciate it." J.D. followed Dewey over to the couch. I went into the kitchen to phone Amos. I could tell by his voice that I woke him, but Amos was first and foremost a protector and defender of the people. If someone needed help, he figured it was his job to respond. Promising to be there as soon as he could, he hung up. I mixed up some more chocolate syrup and milk and then shoved the cup into the microwave.

It felt odd to have J.D. in my house after the evening I'd spent with his wife. I had no intention of mentioning Ina Mae's experience in church. It was her responsibility to tell him about it if she chose to do so. I had to wonder if her marriage had contributed to her problems. J.D. was a nice enough man, always friendly and personable, but sometimes I wondered if his job had become too time-consuming. He seemed rather driven, not only by his profession, but in other ways as well. Once he moved to town, he jumped quickly into what passed for Winter Break's social circle. With a little arm-twisting, he'd wrangled a spot on the city council. I wasn't sure how prestigious the position was since he shared his council spot with Mort Benniker, a local pig farmer whose only claim to fame was that he could burp the alphabet after taking only one breath. But J.D. seemed happy to have a place where he could contribute to the town's future. I certainly couldn't fault him for that.

I'd just removed the cup from the microwave when the phone rang. It was my mother.

"Ivy, my plane leaves at four o'clock this afternoon, my time. I won't get into the Wichita airport until one in the morning on Friday. Are you sure Amos can still pick me up?"

"You know Amos, Mom. He gets by on very little sleep. He says he can do it, but if he gets tired, stop at a motel and rest awhile. There's no rush. I want you both to be safe."

"Is everything all right there? Has anything else happened?"

"No, Mom. No more dead bodies. Dewey's staying with me until you get here, but I don't think I'm in any danger." The missing keys popped into my mind. "But better safe than sorry, I guess."

"Okay, sweetie. See you Friday."

"Bye, Mom." I put the phone down, wishing my parents lived closer. I really missed them. They'd felt the call to China for years. Now they were there, laying their lives down for the gospel. I knew wanting them here was selfish, but I couldn't help it.

I plopped some mini marshmallows into J.D.'s cup and carried it into the living room. He and Dewey were deep in a conversation about the library.

"Why not use the facility in the evenings for book clubs? If we charged a small rental fee, we could use the money toward upkeep and new books," J.D. was saying.

"It's a good idea," Dewey answered. He looked at me when I walked into the room. "Ivy, aren't there a couple of clubs that meet at the bookstore?"

"Yes, the romance club meets once a month, and the Zane Grey club meets every other month. Oh, and Hope and I were talking about a mystery book club. To be honest, though, I have to either drive back into town or stay late to let them in. If you want to move the clubs to the library, it would be fine with me."

"Hope is living at Sarah Johnson's, isn't she?" J.D.

said. "She's much closer to the library than you are to the bookstore."

I nodded and handed him his cup. "It *would* be easier for her to open the library."

He put his hot chocolate down on the coffee table. "Ivy, I'd love to see what you've done with the house. I haven't been here since I closed the deal with Amos."

I started to tell him that things hadn't changed much. Cecil and Marion had left almost all their furniture when they moved to Florida. But I had brought quite a few of Bitty's things in. Her oak antique sideboard sat against one wall of the dining room. Her mother's Blue Willow china was displayed on it. And her oak rocking chair was near a window with her old brass floor lamp next to it. I'd also framed some pictures of Bitty and dedicated a wall to chronicle her life. The guest room held her bedroom furniture. "Sure. I'd be happy to give you a quick tour." I looked at Dewey. "You want to come?"

He shook his head. "I've already seen every room in this house. Right now the only one I care about is the one I'm going to be sleeping in."

"Go on to bed then, Dewey. I'll be fine. J.D. is here, and Amos is on his way. You don't need to stay up with me."

He cocked his head to one side and raised his eyebrows. "You sure?"

I grinned. "I'm certain. I'm suspending your babysitter responsibilities for tonight."

It didn't take much encouragement. He headed toward the stairs. "You'd better show J.D. the upstairs first. I'm going to be sawing logs in the guestroom in a few minutes."

"I think we better take that threat seriously, J.D."

He laughed and we followed Dewey upstairs. I showed J.D. through the upstairs bedrooms, then we went back downstairs. When we reached the dining room, J.D. stopped.

"Ivy, I hope I'm not out of line, but what did you mean by Dewey being your 'babysitter'?"

"You're not out of line. Amos feels that since Dela Shackleford was killed in my driveway, I might be in danger, too. I think he's wrong, but Amos is Amos. When he gets something in his mind, that's it."

J.D. smiled. "Sounds like a man in love."

I'd never really paid much attention to J.D., but I realized that he really was a nice-looking man. His dark brown hair framed an intelligent face, and his eyes were so blue, they almost looked fake. I wondered if he wore colored contacts.

"Yes, he does, doesn't he?"

J.D.'s gaze moved to Marion's tapestry. "It's really something."

"Yes, it is. I love it."

"That's you and Amos, isn't it?" he asked, pointing to the spot where Amos and I held hands and skated on the frozen lake.

"Yes. You know, Marion painted us as a couple. She also painted Buddy and Emily together. Odd, huh?"

He smiled. "Maybe Marion was prophetic. I think it's very special. I hear you're having your wedding reception here. Will you leave the tapestry up?"

"Absolutely. You know, Dela thought it should come down. We would have had a battle over that one." I laughed. "She was about as stubborn as I am. I wonder who would have won."

J.D. walked over to the French doors that led to the deck. Snow was still falling, but it was lighter now. He stared out the window for a few seconds and then shook his head. "I still can't believe she's dead." His voice was soft and there was a hint of pain. The anonymous tip about Dela having an affair popped into my mind, along with the sadness I'd seen in Ina Mae's face. Could it be. . . ?

"I didn't realize you knew Dela and Barney that well."

J.D. turned around. I saw the hurt in his eyes. "I sold their house in Dodge City and helped them find the new one in Winter Break. Ina Mae and I moved here a couple of months before Dela and Barney. A mutual friend referred me to them. During the process, Barney was gone a lot, on the road, you know. I spent most of my time with Dela." He pointed to the dining room table. "Do you mind if we sit down?"

I shook my head. "Of course not. I'll get our hot chocolate." I retrieved our cups and joined him at the table.

"I want you to understand something, Ivy," he said

in slow, measured syllables. "I have never cheated on Ina Mae, but I was attracted to Dela." His eyes went back toward the window. I got the feeling he could say what he had to say more easily if he wasn't looking at me. "We started out talking about the house, but before long, we began sharing other things from our lives." He smiled, but it was empty and melancholy. "Dela was so different from Ina Mae. Vivacious. Interesting. Flamboyant. I found her compelling and. . .challenging." He turned to look at me. "I know how selfish that sounds. I'm really sorry it happened. Especially because Ina Mae got it in her head that Dela and I were actually having an affair." He shook his head. "She started going through my billfold, checking my pockets, even looking through my office for signs that I was cheating on her. It wasn't true, but I couldn't convince her of it. And then one day, she found some jewelry I'd picked up for Dela at an estate sale." His eyes locked on mine. "Dela was always buying jewelry. She liked to find expensive things at estate sales, yard sales, thrift stores. . .you know, places where she could pay a fraction of what they were worth. When Barney was out of town, I'd go with her sometimes. She hid a lot of her purchases from Barney. He's not a selfish guy, but he did ask Dela to show some restraint." He chuckled. "She tried, but it just wasn't in her nature. This one time, she sent me back to pick up a pearl necklace and matching earrings. The guy who was selling them had called her. He wanted to get rid of them and had cut the price in half. She couldn't get them without Barney finding out, so she asked me to keep them for her until she could retrieve them. I had them in my dresser drawer." He stared down at his hands. "I tried to explain it to Ina Mae, but she never would believe me."

"She thought you bought them as a gift for Dela?"

He nodded. "To this day, she thinks I betrayed her. She still doesn't trust me. We don't talk much anymore. To be honest, I've kind of thrown myself into my work. I guess it's so I won't have to deal with the way things are between us."

"Maybe you need to try again. It might be different this time."

"I don't know. She was so angry, Ivy." He looked up at me. "And then when I found out Dela had been murdered. . ."

I didn't know what to say. Did he really think Ina Mae had killed Dela? *Could* she have done it? I thought about her actions at church. Was it absolution she'd been seeking? I had a hard knot in my stomach. "J.D., after you picked Ina Mae up at the church the night of the city council meeting, did you go right home?"

"Yes. I was really tired. I'd been out of town showing two properties. When we got home, I went straight to bed." He stared at me, worry lines creasing his mouth and eyes. "And no, I don't know if Ina Mae left after I went to bed. I just can't believe she could have. . ." He stopped and shook his head. "I've been with Ina Mae for twenty years. She doesn't have a violent bone in her whole body. There's just no way. Really."

I got the distinct feeling J.D. was trying hard to convince both of us that Ina Mae couldn't have killed Dela. But scorned women, whether their rejection was real or imagined, had committed violent acts before. The possibility was obvious, but there was something else working in my mind. The bracelet Dela wore. The reason it was too big. "J.D.," I said, "during your jewelry buying trips with Dela, did you ever see her buy a rhinestone bracelet with blue stones?"

He looked startled. "Can I ask why you're interested in that bracelet?"

I sighed. "You can, but unfortunately for now, I can't answer your question. I can tell you that it's really important. You said 'that bracelet.' Do you know the one I'm talking about?"

He nodded. "I remember it because the family of the woman who sold it to Dela got really upset about it. They said it had been sold for a fraction of its worth."

"What did Dela do about it?"

He shrugged. "She wasn't concerned. She said a deal was a deal. I don't think she was trying to be harsh, but people like Dela are looking for a 'steal' when they go to estate sales. When they find one, they take it. There's just as much risk the other way. You know, buying something you think is valuable and finding out later it's not what you thought it was."

"Did you talk to the people who sold the bracelet yourself?"

"No. Dela told me all about it. She'd gotten several calls from someone related to the original owner. After awhile, the calls began to get scary. Threatening. I insisted she contact the police, but she wouldn't do it. Then she and Barney moved to Winter Break." He smiled. "Not a place most people would think of looking, I guess. Dela never heard from them again." He cupped his hands around his cup as if trying to warm them. "I don't know. At the time Dela's reasoning made sense. Now that I think about it, maybe she should have tried to make it right." He looked at me quizzically. "Does that help you?"

"I'm not sure," I said honestly. "But I appreciate the information. J.D., could Ina Mae have known anything about the bracelet?"

He thought for a moment. "Maybe. She listens in on a lot of my phone calls, although she'd never admit it. I can't really be certain." He took a sip from his cup then he set it down. "You make a great cup of cocoa, and you're a wonderful listener. Sorry I dumped all that on you. Guess I've been stuffing my concerns for so long they were waiting to come out to the first kind person who cared enough to let me talk. I hope I haven't made you uncomfortable."

"Not at all," I said. "My great-aunt Bitty used to say that the difference between a friend and a stranger was a cup of hot chocolate and a good conversation. I'm glad you felt comfortable enough to share your feelings."

He chuckled. "I guess that makes us friends."

"I guess it does," I said with a smile. "Could I make a suggestion, J.D.?"

He nodded. "Of course."

"Why don't you and Ina Mae meet with Pastor Taylor? I'm afraid I'm not an expert on marriage, but Pastor Taylor is a pretty smart man. I think if you two could get honest about your feelings, he could probably help you."

J.D. stared out the window at the snow. "You might be right. I should have suggested it a long time ago. I guess I was just so ashamed of having feelings for Dela. But if admitting my sin in front of my pastor will save my marriage, I'll do it." His gaze shifted to me and he reached over and squeezed my hand. "Thanks, Ivy."

"I really believe you two will be okay," I said. "How about another shot of cocoa?"

He handed me his cup. "I'd love it."

I was on my way to the kitchen when I heard a strange thumping sound. A glance toward the front door revealed the origin. Miss Skiffins was wrapped around one of J.D.'s snow boots.

"Miss Skiffins!" I hollered. "Get away from there!" She rewarded my command by totally ignoring me. I put our cups on the kitchen counter and looked at J.D., who seemed to find the whole thing funny. "I'm really sorry. She has this thing about certain shoes." Up until that moment, she'd been focused on my slippers and a pair of my sneakers. I'd discovered her more than once with her head inside one of them.

Thankfully, she wasn't actually inside one of J.D.'s boots, but she was certainly enamored by them. She had pushed it over and was licking the bottom as if it were her kitten. Luckily, she was enjoying herself so much she didn't run from me when I approached her. It took a little effort to separate her from her new rubber friend, but after a few pulls and some severe scolding, she let go. I carried the small, calico kitten into the kitchen.

"I have no idea what got into her," I said to a very amused J.D. "There's something about your boots she really likes."

"Don't worry about it," he said with a grin. "If I didn't need them tonight, I'd leave them here for her. She certainly enjoys them more than I do."

I set the cat down next to her food bowl in the kitchen. Then I reached into the cabinet for a can of cat food. Usually, that was all it took to get her attention. But as soon as I released her, she made a beeline back to the boots. I ran after her, but she reached her goal before I could scoop her up. Again, she fastened her claws around one of the boots and I had to pry her off. It was really rather embarrassing. J.D.'s hoots of laughter didn't help. Once again, I relieved my obsessed feline from the object of her affection. "You're on a time-out, missy," I scolded. "I'm sorry, J.D. I'll be right back." I ran up the stairs and deposited the cat in one of the bedrooms. "You sit in here and think about your manners," I hissed at her. Unfortunately, she didn't look the least bit repentant. I closed the door and hurried back down the stairs. When I rounded the corner, J.D. was still laughing.

"I'm glad you think it's funny," I said with a smile. "If she's poked a hole in your boot, you might not find it so humorous the next time you step in a puddle."

He waved his hand toward me. "Don't worry about it. I'm actually glad I got stuck in the snow tonight. I've had a wonderful time. Miss Skiffins was simply the entertainment section of our evening."

I noticed that J.D.'s overall appearance had changed since he'd come in the front door. His guarded persona had been replaced with an easy affability. I shook my head and snickered. "I guess it *was* pretty funny. Cats are really unusual animals. They have minds of their own. Seems like dogs work hard to obey you. Cats work twice as hard to ignore you."

J.D. grinned. "I had a cat when I was a kid, and you're right. He was quite a character. Ina Mae and I have two springer spaniels. They're our babies, I guess. Maybe we should add a cat to the mix. I have to admit my dogs aren't nearly as entertaining as your Miss Skiffins."

I'd just made two more cups of hot chocolate when there was a knock on the door. "That should be Amos." I handed him his cup. "You drink that first then we'll take care of your car."

I set my cup down on the table and hurried to the door. When I opened it, I found Amos standing there with an odd look on his face. I could immediately see that something was wrong. He stepped inside and stomped his boots on the carpet without saying a word to me.

"What's the matter, Amos?" I asked. "Has something happened?"

He grabbed my hand and led me into the dining room where J.D. sat sipping from his cup. "J.D.," he said in a somber voice, "I received a call from my dispatcher on my way over here. Your neighbors heard your dogs barking for over an hour, so they went over to your place to see what was wrong. They found Ina Mae at the bottom of your back steps. I'm so sorry, J. D., but she's dead."

10

Amos and J.D. left to go to his house. Emergency medical personnel were still there with Ina Mae's body. Dr. Lucy Barber had also responded. Her practice was in Hugoton, but she came to Winter Break frequently to take care of its citizens. She was also a friend of mine. Amos told me that Lucy determined Ina Mae's death was an unfortunate accident. She had gone outside to check on the dogs and slipped on the icy back stairs and broken her neck. Lucy had already released the body to Elmer Buskins at Buskins Funeral Home, but they were waiting for J.D. to arrive and tell them if he wanted her sent somewhere else. Since the Feldhammers weren't originally from Winter Break, it was possible he would want another mortuary to handle things.

I was tired, but I couldn't sleep. I heated up my cold cup of chocolate and sat at the dining room table where J.D. and I had laughed at Miss Skiffins a little over an hour earlier. I couldn't believe that Ina Mae was dead. It seemed so strange, talking with her at church, and then suddenly, she was gone. All I could do was pray for J.D. Our time together had definitely brought us closer. Odd how a stranger can become a friend in such a short amount of time. Now, his pain was mine. I doubted that I would ever forget the look on his face when Amos told him about his wife. It was as if the bottom had dropped out of his world. And it probably had. I couldn't help but wonder if he was regretting the rift in his marriage and wishing he'd had a chance to repair it.

A movement out near the lake caught my eye. There he was. The collie was trotting around the shore. He stopped and looked my way. I got up and checked the refrigerator. There was some roast beef left from Sunday. I took it out and set it on the cabinet. Then I got my coat and opened the French doors. The dishes I'd left outside for the dog were on the ground next to the deck stairs. As I stepped down the slick stairs to get them, I realized that this was exactly what Ina Mae had done. The thought sent a shiver of alarm through my body. I held on tightly to the stair rail going down and coming back up. On my way back toward the house, I got an idea. There was a small storage shed on the deck where the lawn tools were kept. I unlatched the door, pulled the string for the overhead light, and looked inside. It wasn't big, but there was enough room for a small border collie. I went inside the house and checked out the linen closet. I found an old comforter that I hardly ever used. I put the roast in the food pan and carried it and the comforter out to the shed. Then I took the frozen water bowl to the kitchen and cleaned it out. I put the fresh water in the shed and put a small gardening trowel under the door so that it would remain open a crack. I also left the light on.

If the dog could find enough courage and trust to go inside the shed, he'd be safe from the cold.

I watched from inside until I was finally exhausted enough to go upstairs and try to sleep. Maybe it was thinking about Ina Mae and the look in her eyes before she went up for prayer at the church, but I was determined to help that dog. Ina Mae was certainly more important than an animal, but the border collie had become a symbol for me—that the impossible *was* possible. That there was no one so broken, God couldn't mend them. No creature so hurt that they couldn't be redeemed. Since I'd put the food into the shed, I hadn't seen the dog. It was up to him now. Help was extended. He'd have to decide whether or not to accept it.

I went upstairs and collapsed on my bed. As I lay there, staring up at the ceiling, I realized that a lot of people were in the same condition as the abandoned collie. They felt lost and alone, deserted by the people they'd trusted the most. Yet there was Someone still waiting for them, Someone who had been calling them their whole lives. He was holding out a life full of love, acceptance, and peace, yet because of fear, many of them turned a deaf ear to that call. And just like the small, lost dog, their very lives depended on taking a step of faith out of the cold and into warmth and safety. As I fell asleep, I prayed for the collie and for all the people in the world who had never felt the kind of love that God has for anyone who will simply accept it.

I woke up in the morning to the smell of bacon and coffee. For a moment, I was confused. Then I remembered that Dewey was staying with me. However, bacon wasn't on Dewey's list of approved foods. I got out of bed, pulled on a pair of jeans and a sweatshirt, ran my hands through my hair, and stumbled down the stairs to the kitchen. Dewey was sitting at the kitchen counter, eating oatmeal. Amos was at the stove, cooking bacon and scrambled eggs.

"What are you doing here?" I asked. "And. . .what are you doing?"

"I'm making your breakfast, Sherlock," Amos said with a mocking smile. "Boy, you don't wake up too sharp, do you?"

Dewey didn't say anything, but he chuckled.

"Okay, I guess I deserved that, but *why* are you making my breakfast?"

He put his fork down on the spoon rest next to the stove. Then he came over and put his arms around me. "Because last night I realized how really blessed I am." His voice cracked a little. He stepped back and looked into my eyes. "Watching J.D. come to grips with losing his wife brought me to the conclusion that no matter what happens in life, I can do anything with you by my side." Without any warning, he kissed me.

When he finished, I put my hand up to my mouth. "Shoot and bother, Amos! I haven't even brushed my teeth yet!"

He laughed and kissed me again. "I don't care.

After we're married, I intend to kiss you every morning of your life!"

I stepped away before he could grab me again. "You keep cooking. I'll be back." I ran upstairs to the bathroom, brushed my teeth and my hair, and put on some mascara. By the time I got back, Amos was putting my food on a plate. Before I sat down, I checked outside. I could hardly believe what I saw. Sticking out of the tool shed was the tip of a black tail. I resisted the urge to go out there. I kept my mouth shut and went back to the kitchen. It wasn't that I was trying to keep my progress with the dog from Amos. Okay, yes, I was. For now, I thought it would be best to keep it to myself.

"Amos told me about Ina Mae," Dewey said when I sat down on the stool at the counter. "I can't believe it. We just saw her last night. It doesn't seem real."

I prayed over my food and then stuck a forkful of eggs in my mouth. "I know," I said after I swallowed. I was hungrier than I'd expected, and the eggs were delicious. "I can't imagine what J.D. is going through today. First Barney and now J.D. It's terrible."

"I thought maybe we'd go by and see him," Amos said. He'd fixed himself a plate but ate it standing up, leaning against the counter in the kitchen. "Milton Baumgartner and his sons were already out this morning, clearing Main Street. You can go to the bookstore for a while if you want to, and we can stop by J.D.'s on the way home."

Milton Baumgartner ran Winter Break's volunteer fire department. He also owned a farm outside of town. Milton and his sons were always the first ones out after a snowfall, cleaning the snow from our downtown streets.

"Sounds like a good idea," I said. "Are you going with us, Dewey?"

The old man nodded. "I'd really like to open the store. When it snows like this, folks like to stock up." He stood up and pushed the kitchen stool to the side. "If it won't cause any trouble, I'd like to get a quick shower first. Besides," he said, "I'd rather not watch you two shovel down bacon and scrambled eggs."

I grinned at him. "I understand. Go ahead. I'll get a shower when you're done. Don't use up all the hot water."

He shot me a dirty look. "Thanks for giving me ideas. Perhaps the cold water will stir up your sense of compassion. Next time you can eat oatmeal with me."

"Oatmeal?" Amos said with a smirk. "Only old people eat oatmeal."

Dewey wadded up his napkin and threw it, bouncing it perfectly off Amos's forehead, making us all laugh. As soon as Dewey went up the stairs, I said, "I've got so much to tell you!"

"Me, too," Amos said. "You go first."

I told him about J.D.'s interest in Dela and how suspicious Ina Mae had been of her husband's activities.

He set his plate down next to the sink and folded

his arms across his chest. "Are you saying he thinks Ina Mae killed Dela?"

"He didn't say that, Amos. In fact, he defended her. But I could tell the thought had crossed his mind."

"I wonder if she could have taken Dela's bracelet. Maybe she hid it somewhere in her house." He reached over and poured himself a cup of coffee. He held out the pot to me but I shook my head. I'd barely started on my first cup.

"Not if the bracelet Hope has is the one we're looking for."

Amos rubbed his temples. "Here we go again. You know, we've faced a few confusing situations, but we've never tackled anything with so many rabbit trails. I start down one, and another one pops up. I can't seem to find a clear path."

I took a big sip of coffee. The jolt of caffeine helped to wake me up a little. "Well, what do we have so far? I mean, we know I didn't do it."

Amos grinned. "You know, if you'd just confess, we could wrap this up. I'm really tired of thinking about it."

"You're very funny. Will you please try to concentrate?"

He threw his hands up in a gesture of surrender.

"We think Hope has the bracelet," I said slowly, "but there's nothing to tie her to Dela. And as far as this 'affair' tip you got, the only affair seems to be one that was in J.D.'s mind, and according to him, it never went anywhere. The only real motive we've come up with so far belongs to Ina Mae. She thought her husband was having an affair with Dela. But if she did it, what about the bracelet? You know, this bracelet doesn't seem to fit anywhere. It's confusing." I took another sip then put my cup down. "Anything from the KBI yet?"

Amos shook his head. "They're going over the car, but so far the only fingerprints they've found are yours, Dela's, and Barney's. It's a new car, so any other prints could belong to the killer. And the only fingerprints on the chopstick are yours and Dela's. Of course, we already expected that." He sighed. "The recurring theme here seems to be you."

"Obviously the killer wore gloves," I murmured.

"I'd like to suggest that you start wearing gloves," Amos grumbled. "It would certainly solve a lot of problems."

I chose to ignore him. "Do you think the sheriff still suspects me?"

"I don't know. If he really thought you'd done it, you'd be behind bars. But it's not over yet, Ivy. He still has to follow the clues, and right now they point toward you. And here's the newest information—and this only adds to the puzzle. Remember the tip that mentioned Barney and insurance fraud?"

"Yes?"

Amos sighed again and absentmindedly ran his hand through his hair. "There may be some truth to it."

I almost dropped my fork. "What are you talking about?"

"Barney's company didn't send him to western Kansas just because he needed to be closer to his clients. There were some suspicions about a couple of properties that burned down. The owners increased their coverage through Barney, and then suddenly, the buildings went up in smoke. One was a restaurant in Dodge City that wasn't doing very well. Another was a farm belonging to a guy who lived a few miles outside the city. Seems he was getting ready to lose everything. He increases his coverage, and his house and outbuildings burn down." He shrugged. "There wasn't any clear evidence of wrongdoing, so the company paid, but the suspicion was so strong, the top dogs wanted to distance themselves from Barney. They couldn't fire him without proof, so moving him out here was the only answer they could come up with."

"But what does that have to do with Dela's death?"

"If Dela knew Barney was getting payoffs from his clients, he could have killed her to shut her up. Maybe she was planning to turn him in."

"So he stabbed her with a bronze chopstick from their wedding? Really good plan." Actually, for the first time, I realized how using the chopstick had a twisted justice to it. Barney in the dragon suit flashed in my mind. Could he have endured a ceremony like that and then killed the woman he was willing to humiliate himself for?

"Unfortunately, that's not all. Barney recently took out a large life insurance policy on Dela. He stands to rake in a million dollars."

"A million dollars?" I could hardly believe it. Things were certainly piling up against Barney.

"Of course, if he killed Dela, he'll never see the money."

I drank some more coffee, trying to clear the cobwebs out of my head. "But what would the bracelet have to do with anything? Barney didn't need to steal it. He could have gotten it anytime he wanted to. And why kill her in a car in my driveway? It would have been easier somewhere else." I thought for a moment. "You know something, Amos? Those chopsticks bother me."

"What do you mean?"

"How could anyone know she had them in her purse? Originally, they were in her attaché case. And who would even know she had them in the first place, or had moved them to her purse, except me? If you plan to kill someone, you're not going to hope they have a pair of chopsticks in their purse. You're going to bring a weapon with you. It doesn't make any sense."

"From what you've just told me, I have even more reason to think you did it."

I shot him a dirty look.

"I'm starting to wonder if this bracelet is getting us off track," he said. "If we take it out of the equation, things look a lot clearer."

"But we can't forget about it. Dela had it on when she was alive. When she was dead, it was gone. Now Hope may have it. We've got to follow that rabbit trail.

Even if it leads us the wrong way."

"I guess we just add it to everything else." Amos finished his eggs and rinsed off his dish. Then he picked up the frying pan and dumped a large amount of scrambled eggs into a bowl which he set in front of me.

"Thanks, but I'm full. Are you trying to fatten me up so I can't possibly fit into my wedding dress, should I ever have one?"

He came around the counter and kissed me on the head. "No. I thought maybe your toolshed guest might like them."

My mouth dropped open. "You know about that?"

"When I got here, I looked out the back windows to see if the snow had stopped. I saw him looking out the door."

"Did he see you?"

"No. I stepped back before he noticed me." Amos's face crinkled in a frown. "I understand what you're trying to do, Ivy. But I mean it about being careful. Don't approach him. You let him come to you—if he ever does. This might be as close as he'll ever get. You understand that, right?"

I smiled and nodded. Of course I didn't understand it. *Nothing so broken that God can't mend it.*

He shook his head like he knew what I was thinking. "I'm going to talk to Hope about that bracelet. Then I've got to ask Barney about the fraud allegations. I'll come back as soon as I can to get you and Dewey."

"Amos, my mom called. She's getting into Wichita about one in the morning."

His expression didn't change, but his eyes widened for a second. "No problem."

"I don't think you should do it. You have too much going on. I'll get her."

"Hey, now that's a good idea. Or, we could just go out and push your car into a snowdrift and get it over with." He wrapped his arms around me. "Don't worry about it. We're a team. I'll get your mother. Everything will be fine." He leaned down to kiss me. "You get your shower. I'll be back as soon as I can." He started to walk away, then he stopped and turned around. "And say a prayer for me, will you? There's no way I can ask Barney these questions without making it obvious he's a suspect. That's not something I really want to do."

"I will. Amos, maybe you should take me with you to talk to Hope. You know, because I'm a woman. It might make things easier."

He took his coat off the rack. "Yes, I've noticed you're a woman." He slid on his coat and paused with his hand on the door. "You know what? Maybe I'll take you with me on both visits. You haven't had a chance to offer Barney your condolences, and I could use your insight. Maybe you could make him your famous tuna casserole. But, Ivy," he said, frowning at me, "let me ask the questions, okay? I don't want it to get back to Hitchens that you're interrogating witnesses."

I nodded at him and smiled. I knew Amos wanted

my help, but his "official side" had boundaries. It was my job to try not to step over them. I was going to have to keep my nosiness in check.

"Why don't you get ready, and I'll pick you and Dewey up around noon. I want to see how the snow removal's going, and I need to stop by Dorian Harker's place. Seems he loaned his camper to Pete Bennett so his brother could stay in it until he got a job and found a place to live. He moved out a couple of months ago and no one told Dorian." A slow smile spread across his face. "I guess the door was left open and a family of raccoons moved in. He's got a camper full of raccoon droppings and he's fit to be tied." He shook his head and chortled. "Who ever said the life of a deputy sheriff isn't glamorous?"

I didn't envy Amos his raccoon detail, but I was thrilled to go with him. I wanted to hear what Barney and Hope had to say. Maybe we'd uncover our murderer today. Although, I had to admit that neither one of them seemed like good suspects to me. "Thanks, Amos. I'll be ready."

He blew me a kiss and went out the door. I really was concerned about the long trip to Wichita. Amos wasn't getting much sleep. I wondered if there was another way to get my mother here. I decided to look up bus schedules when I got to the bookstore. I doubted that she would care. She and my dad frequently used public transportation in Hong Kong. They were constantly utilizing buses, trams, or mass transit. Although I knew there weren't any buses to Winter Break, maybe we could at least get her close.

Dewey was still upstairs taking a shower so I had a little extra time. I carried the eggs outside, but the shed was empty. All the roast beef was gone and most of the water. The water that remained was frozen. The comforter had obviously been slept on. I emptied the eggs into the food bowl and carried the water bowl into the house. After filling it with fresh water, I put it back in the shed. I looked around for the dog but didn't see him. As I closed the French door, I thought I saw something black moving in the yard, on the side of the deck where I couldn't get a clear view. I walked away from the doors so he wouldn't see me and get spooked.

I was rinsing our dishes and putting them in the dishwasher when I noticed the box of honey and jelly Amos had carried in the night before. Since I had a little time, I decided to take it downstairs. First I took one of the jars of jelly out and set it on the counter. I had some in the refrigerator, but it was almost gone. I was addicted to huckleberry jelly. Hopefully, Alma would keep it coming. Every year she visited her sister in Oregon and together they put up jelly and preserves. She even brought back whole huckleberries for baking. I tried to pace myself so I wouldn't run out before the next trip, but it wasn't easy.

The box wasn't too heavy, but after I switched on the basement light, I held on tightly to the stair rail with one hand and the box with the other. The stairs were pretty unstable and needed to be replaced. I made it down to the bottom and carried the box over to the shelves that lined the wall. They reached almost to the ceiling. The shelves were wide and deep and anchored to thick wood backs. Cecil had built them for Marion's peach preserves and homemade applesauce, and he hadn't taken any chances that the shelves would ever break and lose their precious cargo. Marion's peach preserves were fantastic, and she made the best applesauce I'd ever tasted. In the final steps she added red-hot candies. It gave the sauce a wonderful flavor. I'd promised myself that someday I'd learn how to make it just the way she had. For now, though, the shelves were lined with jars of Bubba Weber's honey. I was really happy that Dewey was clearing out one of his storerooms so the honey would finally have a permanent home.

I put the box on top of my washer, then I took the jars of honey from the box and lined them up next to the fifty or sixty other jars we already had. When I finished, I took out the remaining three jars of jelly. When I put them next to the other jars, I got a surprise. And it wasn't a good one. I was certain I'd had five jars left from the last batch Alma gave me. But there were only four. I stood there for a moment trying to remember if I'd counted wrong, but I was sure I hadn't. Could Amos have taken a jar upstairs? I'd checked the fridge yesterday. I was sure there was only a partial jar there. I looked around the room and checked the rest of the shelves to see if a jar had been inadvertently moved, but there was no missing jelly to be found.

"Well, shoot and bother," I said out loud. It wasn't going to do any good to stand here and stare at the remaining jars. I was pretty sure another jar of huckleberry jelly wasn't going to magically appear.

Finally, I picked up the empty box and took it over to the big trash can in the corner. I tossed it in and started to leave when something caught my eye. I got down on my knees and looked under the shelf that held the jelly. A piece of broken glass was lodged under the bottom shelf. I carefully pulled it out. It was part of a jelly jar. Amos must have broken one and not told me. I tossed the glass in the trash can. Although I thought it a little odd he hadn't mentioned it, he was probably just afraid to get between me and my huckleberry jelly. It was actually kind of funny. I made a vow to lighten up on my huckleberry jelly obsession. It was obviously frightening my future husband.

By the time I got upstairs, Dewey was helping himself to a cup of coffee, and behind his back Miss Skiffins was helping herself to the jar of jelly I'd left on the counter. She was licking the jar with all her might, hoping, I guess, that she would eventually wear the glass down and make her way to the prize inside.

"Miss Skiffins!" I yelled. Dewey almost jumped out of his shoes. "Sorry," I said while I chased the chastised cat off my counter. "There was an act of larceny being perpetrated on my huckleberry jelly jar while you weren't watching."

"Next time maybe you could warn an old man who lives alone before you scream at your cat—or anything else," he said, shaking his head. "No one ever yells at my house. I'm not used to it."

I came around the counter and hugged him. "Again, sorry. Maybe you should get a cat. That way you could spend half your time shouting at it to stay out of things. It seems to be an integral part of sharing your life with someone of the feline persuasion."

"I think I'll pass," he said. "My heart doesn't need all the excitement."

I told him about Amos picking us up around noon. Then I put a tuna casserole together and popped it in the oven. By the time I'd showered and changed, Amos was back. I made some sandwiches, took the casserole out of the oven, and we all piled into Amos's car. First we dropped Dewey off at his store, and then we went to the library. Barney's house was a little way out of town, just like mine, except in the opposite direction. Amos wanted to go to Barney's after the library and stop by J.D.'s on the way home. I was wondering how much time I would actually spend in Miss Bitty's Bygone Bookstore today.

The light was on in the library. I was rather certain Hope would be there since Sarah Johnson's house was only a couple of blocks away, but I doubted that Faith had come in. Inez Baumgartner's place was not too far from mine and the roads were still snow-packed. Amos knocked on the door and Hope peeked out. Sure enough, when we stepped inside, there wasn't any sign of Faith.

"I figured you wouldn't venture out today, Ivy," Hope said. "If the sidewalks hadn't been cleared, I'd probably still be at Sarah's." She wrinkled her turned-up nose. "It's really cold out there. How about a cup of coffee?"

"No thanks," Amos said, speaking for both of us.

"Actually, I'd love a cup," I said, sitting down in the chair by the door. "Thanks, Hope." When she left to get the coffee, I poked Amos in the side. "The more relaxed you make this, the more information you'll get, Deputy," I whispered. "Don't give her the third degree, just talk to her."

He bent over and put his mouth near my ear. "You're not actually a law enforcement officer, Ivy," he whispered. "I know my job."

I squeezed his arm. "I know you do, cutie pie, but cleaning out raccoon excrement doesn't really qualify you for interrogation, does it?"

"First of all, I didn't clean out raccoon excrement. I just told Pete Bennett to do it. And secondly, don't call me cutie pie." He sounded mad but I saw him trying to hide a smile.

Hope came back into the room carrying my coffee. After handing it to me, she leaned against the nearby desk. "Now what can I do for you two?" she asked.

Amos pulled out his notepad. "Hope, I need to ask you something. It's about a bracelet. . ."

Hope's eyes widened. "A bracelet? How would you know about that?"

I jumped in before Amos could answer. If there was any way to keep Faith out of this, I wanted to do it. "Someone saw it, Hope. It doesn't matter who it was. They just happened to mention it."

She looked confused. "I don't understand why it would be important to you."

Amos cleared his throat. "It's important because Dela Shackleford was wearing a rhinestone bracelet in the morning, but when we found her body that night, it was gone. We need to know what happened to it. If you have it, I need you to explain to me how it came into your possession."

The color drained from Hope's face. "Are you saying you suspect me of killing Dela Shackleford?" She slumped against the desk. For a moment, I was afraid she was going to faint.

I shot a look of warning to Amos. "No, of course not. No one thinks you had anything to do with her murder. Amos just needs to tie up all the loose ends. It's part of his job."

Hope glanced from me at Amos. "The bracelet isn't rhinestones, Amos. It's made out of diamonds and sapphires. It's worth almost seven thousand dollars."

Now I was the one who felt faint. This information certainly didn't make Hope look innocent. She'd just given herself a motive for murder. "Is it the same bracelet I saw Dela wearing Wednesday morning?" I asked.

Hope nodded. "Yes, it is."

"Can you tell me how you gained possession of it?" Amos asked.

Since he was ignoring my advice and talking in his official *deputy sheriff* voice, I jumped in. "You're not in any trouble," I said with a smile. "I'm sure there's a simple explanation."

She pulled herself up onto the desk, her legs dangling over the side. "I'm afraid the explanation isn't that simple, Ivy. Dela came by here Wednesday afternoon and gave it to me."

Even I had a hard time accepting that. Amos's expression was one of pure skepticism. "Why would she give you a bracelet worth seven thousand dollars?" I asked.

She shrugged. "That's simple. Because it's mine." She folded her arms in front of her. "Look, it belonged to my grandmother. After she first became ill, I moved in to help her. But eventually, she got so bad I couldn't give her proper care. We put an ad in the local paper so we could sell some of her things and hopefully get enough money for her move to a nursing home. The only item she had that was really valuable was the bracelet. At first, she didn't want to sell it. But once she realized how dire things really were, she agreed to let it go. I told her that I would take it to someone who could get us a good price for it. Like a professional jeweler or collector. But one afternoon while I was out, a woman came by inquiring about the jewelry. My grandmother, who had Alzheimer's, sold her the bracelet for two hundred dollars. When I returned home and found out, I was frantic. Thank goodness the woman had left her name and number in case there were any more pieces my grandmother wanted to sell."

"It was Dela?" I asked.

She nodded. "Yes. I called her several times, asking her to return the bracelet, but she kept putting me off."

"Why didn't you call the police?" I asked.

"It wouldn't have done any good," Amos said. "The bracelet wasn't stolen. The only thing she could have done would have been to take Dela to court."

"That's right," Hope said. "Unless the court decided that my grandmother wasn't competent to make the deal she had, we had no case. Alzheimer's is kind of like a roller coaster. Some days were good, some were bad. If they questioned her on a good day, she would have sounded completely rational." She sighed. "I didn't know what to do. I guess I should have pursued it, but then my grandmother died, and I gave up."

"Until you found out Dela was living in Winter Break?" Amos asked.

"Yes. I didn't know her by sight, but I certainly knew her name. When she was introduced to me as someone interested in the library, I was shocked, to say the least. She obviously didn't remember my name. A couple of days after that, I went to see her. I told her who I was and explained how much I needed that bracelet. You see, there wasn't enough money to pay for all the funeral expenses, and I had to take out a loan. Making the payments has been very difficult. My grandmother had a few other debts that passed to me. I have to find a way to pay them off. My only choice is to sell the bracelet."

"Look, Hope," I said slowly, "I don't want to cast aspersions on Dela when she can't defend herself, but why would she suddenly decide to give you back the bracelet? It doesn't sound like her."

"You may find this hard to believe, but she told me that once I'd put a face to the situation, she couldn't keep the bracelet. She even apologized for not making things right sooner. And she wouldn't even let me pay her back the two hundred dollars. Dela turned out to be a much nicer person than I'd imagined her to be."

"Where's the bracelet now?" Amos asked.

"It's in my room at Sarah's. I planned to get a safety deposit box in Hugoton, but then the weather got so bad." A look of panic swept across her face. "You aren't going to take it, are you?"

"Well, not yet," Amos said solemnly, "but I can't guarantee that the sheriff won't order me to confiscate it at some point. It may be evidence. If we do take it, it will be safe, and if it's determined that it has nothing to do with Dela's murder, it will be returned to you."

Hope slid off the desk and stood in front of him. "You don't believe me, do you? You really think I'm involved in this somehow." Her voice has harsh with resentment.

"I'm not forming an opinion one way or the other. It's not my job. I'm only trying to find out what happened to Delaphine Shackleford. I think her killer should be brought to justice, don't you?" The glint in his narrowed eyes went toe to toe with Hope's determined expression. I wasn't sure who was winning, but I felt it was time to call a truce.

"Amos, we need to get going. That casserole I made for Barney is going to be frozen solid if we don't get it to him soon." I stood up and stepped between them, giving Hope a hug. "I'm sure everything will be okay. Please don't worry. We'll find the truth, I'm sure of it."

Hope didn't really hug me back, she just stood there. But at least she didn't pull away. I said good-bye, then steered Amos out the front door. When we stepped out on the sidewalk, he broke my grip on his arm.

"Why did you do that, Ivy? There were a few other things I wanted to ask her."

"Let's get in the car. She was getting angry, Amos. And frightened. Do you want her to skip town? If she really is involved, you'd have to find her. I don't think you want to do that."

"You can't interfere when I'm questioning a suspect. I asked for your insight, not your interference."

I knew I'd crossed over the line. "I'm sorry. I really was only trying to calm her down. I'll watch it."

He shook his head and helped me down the steps to the car. We climbed inside and he started the engine.

After staring out the window for several seconds he turned towards me. "I accept your apology, Ivy. I know this is hard on you. I really want your help, but I have to be careful. You're not a law enforcement official. You can't do my job for me. From now on, let me take the lead, okay?"

"I will, I promise,"

The tightness around his jaw relaxed a little. "Do you really believe that story about Dela giving her back the bracelet?" he asked. "Doesn't sound right to me."

"No, it doesn't. But to be honest, neither one of us really knew Dela. I mean, we can't actually *know* someone unless we've really spent some quality time with them, can we?"

"That's sounds good. Now tell me what your gut instinct says."

I sighed deeply. "It is extremely suspicious of Hope's story."

He put the car in gear. "Let's go see Barney. And could you please let me do my job without interrupting?"

I batted my eyelashes at him. "If you'd do your job correctly, I wouldn't have to interrupt."

Amos mumbled something under his breath that I didn't catch. For the sake of our relationship, I decided to let it go.

About fifteen minutes later, we pulled up in front of Barney's house. There were a couple of other cars parked there. I got the casserole out of the back seat and followed Amos to the front door. A woman I'd never seen before opened it to let us in.

Amos introduced himself and asked if Barney was available. The woman took my casserole and led us into the back of the house. Barney was seated in the family room and there were several other people with him.

"Amos and Ivy," he said when we walked in. "How nice of you to come by." He introduced us to each of his relatives. His brother and sister-in-law from Dodge City, his cousin from Missouri, and Dela's sister and brother. Dela's sister looked a lot like her, but she was younger and not as flashy. I felt bad for her. I'd never had a sister, but I could imagine that losing one must be terrible.

"Barney, I hate to bother you at a time like this, but could I talk to you for a few minutes?" Amos asked politely.

"Of course you can," Barney said, rising to his feet. "Let's go into the living room."

I told everyone how nice it had been to meet them and followed Amos and Barney into the other room. The living room was toward the front of the house. Dela's touch was apparent. The décor was modern and rather unconventional for Winter Break, Kansas. But all in all, it was attractive and well put together. I couldn't help comparing Dela's style to mine. Everything in Dela's house was *coordinated. Eclectic* was the only way to describe my home, but I liked the way everything went together. It was comfortable and homey.

Amos and I sat down on a white sofa with zebra-striped throw pillows. Barney sat next to us on a sleek black leather chair. A large, square glass coffee table was in front of us. The walls were painted a warm raspberry, and they were lined with black-framed black-and-white pictures of Barney and Dela. A shiny black piano was against one wall. I wondered if Dela had played. There was so much about her I didn't know.

"Now, what can I do for you, Amos? Have you found out who killed my wife?"

I caught myself comparing Barney's chubby face with that of a shih tzu. I was going to have to stop the dog versus people comparisons. My similes were in bad need of revamping.

"I'm sorry, Barney. We haven't arrested anyone yet, but we're trying hard to get at the truth. Unfortunately, I have to ask you some questions now that won't be comfortable, but I assure you that the only reason I'm asking is so we can eliminate everything that isn't important." Amos took his notepad and pencil out of his pocket and handed them to me. I was surprised but more than happy to help. Maybe Amos was trying to seem a little less official this time around.

"I think I understand," Barney said, looking back and forth between us. "What can I possibly tell you that will help?"

Amos cleared his throat. I knew this was difficult for him. He was connecting to Barney in a way he hadn't with Hope. I felt strongly that I should be quiet and let him find his own way.

"We've received some tips at the office," Amos said carefully. "I want you to know that although we have to follow up on all of them, we don't take anonymous tips too seriously. People call and leave information for a lot of reasons. Some calls are from people who have nothing better to do than to waste our time. Then there are others who have their own axes to grind."

"What are you trying to say, Amos?" Barney said with a frown. "Has someone called in with a tip about my wife's murder?"

"More than one, I'm afraid." Amos leaned forward and clasped his hands together. "Look, Barney, here it is. Just remember, I'm not asking you about these things because I believe them. I'm asking you because it may lead us to Dela's killer."

Barney's face relaxed a bit. "Okay. I understand. Please tell me what these people had to say."

Amos leaned back, clearly relieved that Barney was receptive. "Well, one person said Ivy killed Dela because she wanted to be president of the library board."

Barney's eyes widened and he laughed. "That's ridiculous. Are they all like that?"

Amos nodded. "Pretty much. Someone else claimed that Dela was having an affair and her lover killed her. Another claimed that she was killed over the missing bracelet I told you about. And someone else claimed that you killed her because you were trying to hide some kind of insurance fraud."

I noticed that Amos had left out the accusation about Barney being the killer because of jealousy over an affair. I guess one allegation of murder was enough. I also noticed that his face turned an even pastier white than usual. Because Amos had lumped all of the accusations together, I wasn't certain which one had hit its mark, but unless I missed my guess, at least one of them had caused a definite reaction.

"What can you tell me about these charges, Barney?" Amos asked gently.

"I–I'm flabbergasted," he answered haltingly. "How could anyone think that Dela was cheating on me? It–it's just cruel. And completely untrue." He began to cry. And I don't mean a little bit. He boo-hooed so loudly, the woman who'd opened the front door for us came running into the room.

"Barney! What's the matter? Do you need—"

"I'm all right, Irma," he blubbered. "Leave us alone. Please."

Irma shot Amos and me a dirty look. I immediately felt defensive. As if I'd personally attacked Barney during his most vulnerable moment. All I could do was offer her a sickly smile and shrug my shoulders. When she left, I got up and sat next to him.

"It's okay," I said as soothingly as I could. "It's probably just someone who didn't know you and Dela. Please don't be so upset." I patted his arm and waited for him to get control of himself. I really *did* feel bad for him.

"I'm sorry," he said when his sobs lessened enough for us to understand him. "I guess I never could understand why someone as wonderful as Dela would love someone like me." He shook his head and gave me a small, sad smile. "Believe me, I know I'm not a catch. Dela was so. . .so. . .wonderful. She was the toast of the town in Dodge City, you know. Everyone knew her. I was just the man who followed her around, living in her glory." He reached into his pocket and took out a handkerchief. He wiped his eyes. "But you know what? She truly loved me. The Dela the public saw wasn't the Dela I knew. She was kind and thoughtful. And as silly as it sounds, she was crazy about me. I know that sounds almost impossible, but it's true."

"What about the other charges?" Amos asked cautiously. "Can you tell me anything helpful about them? Is there anyone you think might have made them?"

Barney shook his head. "There were a couple of instances in Dodge City that looked suspicious. People who insured through me and had fires not long after that. But if they were scams to get insurance money, I had nothing to do with it. I know someone at our agency cast aspersions on me, but it wasn't true. There was never any evidence. If there had been, I would have been fired." He thought for a few moments. "And as I told you just the other day, I don't remember the bracelet you described. It doesn't mean that Dela didn't have it at one time. She may have. I showed you Dela's jewelry collection the other day. It's very large. I couldn't keep track of all the pieces. I'm afraid I'd scolded her more than once about buying so much. I'm pretty sure she didn't tell me about everything she purchased."

"We found the bracelet," I said. "Hope Hartwell at the library has it. Can you think of any reason Dela would give her jewelry?"

"No, but it doesn't mean she didn't do it. Dela loved to give jewelry as presents." He suddenly straightened up. "Oh, my goodness. I'm so glad you reminded me." He stood up. "Please, wait here. I'll be right back."

After he left the room, Amos wagged his finger at me. "I'm not sure we should have told Barney about Hope. We're going to have to follow up with her, and I'd rather not have everyone knowing we suspect her."

"I know," I said in a low voice, keeping an eye out for Irma. "But if he had given us a connection between Hope and Dela, it might have made Hope's story more believable."

"What about Dela having an affair? He sure reacted to that."

"Yes, he did," I said. "If he was so secure in his relationship, would he have gotten so emotional? I'm not sure. But I have to say, Dela certainly seemed devoted to him."

He raised his eyebrows. "I hate to say it, but people cheat sometimes even though they claim to love their spouses. I don't think we can rule Barney out."

I started to bring up J. D. Feldhammer again. If

Dela was going to cheat with anyone, why not him? He was certainly good-looking enough. I'd just opened my mouth to share my thoughts when I heard a door close. Barney was on his way back.

"I found it right away," he said as he walked back into the room. "Dela had put it on top of the dresser with this note."

He handed me a long black case. I opened it to find a beautiful emerald green necklace with a matching bracelet and earrings. The deep green baguettes on the necklace and bracelet were edged with sparkling rhinestones set in silver. The earrings were slightly curved with three large green stones in the middle and small rhinestones on each side. The set was breathtaking.

"I'm sorry, Barney," I said. "I don't understand."

"Read the card," he said, his eyes tearing up again. "It will explain everything."

I opened up the envelope he'd handed me. Dela's perfume drifted up from inside. I pulled out the ivory card and read:

Dearest Ivy,

I've noticed how lovely you look in green. I thought perhaps this set would bring out your gorgeous red hair and green eyes. Please accept it from me as your "something old." These pieces actually belonged to my mother. I can't think of anyone else I'd rather see wear them. Thank you for letting me be a part of your wedding. Your friendship has been a tremendous blessing. Your friend, Dela.

Now my own eyes were tearing up. "Oh, Barney, she wanted to loan these to me for my wedding?"

He shook his head vigorously. "No, no, Ivy. She wanted you to have them. They're yours. But please, if you don't like them, don't feel under obligation to wear them. Dela's taste could be somewhat extravagant. This might not be something you'd wear. . ."

"Nonsense," I sputtered, tears running down my face. "They're absolutely beautiful. I'd be honored to wear them. But I don't think I should keep them. Maybe someone in the family. . ."

Barney wiped his eyes and smiled. "To be honest," he said, his voice lowered so only Amos and I could hear him, "Dela couldn't stand my family much, and she despised hers even more. But she thought the world of you. If you don't take this gift, she will probably come back to haunt both of us." He reached over and took my hand in his. "Please, Ivy. I know it would mean so much to Dela, and it would mean a lot to me, too."

I was so overcome with emotion, I could only nod. I hugged Barney and noticed Irma peeking from around the corner to see what was going on. "Okay," I whispered in Barney's ear. "I'll wear these at my wedding as long as you're there to see me in them."

He released me. "I would love to be there. Thank

you, Ivy. And I believe this is for you also." He picked up the folder he'd carried in with the jewelry box. "I believe these are sketches Dela was working on for you."

"Thank you. I'm going to make certain Dela's ideas are incorporated. It will make our special day even more memorable." I slid the file into my purse.

Amos cleared his throat and I turned around to see him frowning at me. I suppose I wasn't being very *professional*, but I didn't really care.

"We need to get going, Barney," he said. "Thank you for giving us your time. If I hear anything helpful, I'll contact you."

"Do you have any idea when they will release Dela?" Barney asked. "It's hard to plan her funeral without knowing. . ."

"I'm sorry," Amos said. "The coroner should release the bod—I mean, Dela, any day now. As soon as I hear something, I'll let you know immediately. Where are you having the funeral?"

"Right here in Winter Break," Barney said. "You know, even though Dela was well known in Dodge City, she never really felt at home there. Everyone was so kind to her here, she was beginning to feel as if she finally belonged somewhere. Helping you with your wedding was the icing on the cake, Ivy. And being chosen to serve on the library board meant the world to her. One consolation I have is that the night Dela died, she was very happy. I love it here, too. I intend to stay, and I want her nearby."

Amos shook his hand and I hugged him again. As we left, weasel-faced Irma watched us all the way to the front door. I was certain she was staring at the jewelry box in my hands, but I didn't feel bad. For some reason, I was happy she wouldn't be getting her hands on it.

"Well, what do you think?" Amos said as soon as we got in the car.

I sighed and stared out the window at the house where Dela had once lived. "I have to tell you, Amos, we've questioned every possible suspect, and I have absolutely no idea who killed Dela Shackleford. After talking to Barney, I realize that I didn't know Dela at all. I thought she hated Winter Break, and I didn't think she was too crazy about me either." I stared at the jewelry box in my hands. "I guess I was wrong."

Amos started the car and turned toward me. "We have too many leads. I can't separate one from the other." He rubbed his gloves together. "I'm going to drop you off at the bookstore for a while. Then we'll visit J.D. on the way home. I've got to go to the office and see if anything new has popped up with this case or with our bank robber. Hopefully, someone else has had more luck than we've had."

He put the car in gear and drove slowly toward town. I couldn't shake a feeling that we were missing something. That the answer was in front of us, but we weren't seeing it. I prayed that God would give us wisdom and that Dela's killer would be brought to justice. For now, I was going on pure faith. A scripture in Proverbs three jumped into my mind: *Trust in the Lord with all your heart and lean not on your own understanding; in all your ways acknowledge him, and he will make your paths straight.*

"Lord," I whispered, "if we ever needed You to make the path straight, this is it. Please help us to put all the pieces together. We can't do it by ourselves. I'm putting my trust in You." A sense of peace washed over me, and by the time we got to the bookstore, I felt like a big burden had been lifted.

As soon as Amos dropped me off at the bookstore, I got on my computer and began looking up bus schedules. I hadn't taken my laptop home yesterday or I could have looked up the information I needed last night. I was going to have to break down and put a computer in the house. I'd been putting it off, but it was no longer a luxury. It was becoming a necessity. I waited for what seemed forever for dial-up service, the only option right now for Winter Break. It took awhile for me to discover that there was no bus that would get my mother close enough to make a difference, but I found a train that could get my mom from Newton, which wasn't too far from Wichita, to Dodge City. It would take Amos only two hours to get to Dodge City. A much better prospect. The problem was that I had no way to call my mother. She was already on her way. I phoned an old friend of the family in Wichita. A deacon at our former church, he was happy to hear from me and perfectly willing to pick up my mother at the airport and drive her to Newton, even though her train wouldn't leave until three thirty in the morning. After speaking to him, I ordered her ticket. It would be waiting for her when she arrived at the train station.

With that problem solved, I packed up some books for mailing, but I could look across the street and see that the post office wasn't open. Alma lived even farther out of town than I did. I was pretty sure she wouldn't venture in to work until tomorrow. Maybe. Oh, the joys of small town living.

It was after five o'clock before Amos finally made it back. I called J.D. to see if it was okay to stop by. He seemed pleased to have company. He was even happier when I offered to stop by Ruby's and pick up dinner. On the way over to Ruby's, I told Amos about putting my mother on a train. Although he had been a trooper about picking her up in Wichita, the difference between a twelve-hour and a four-hour round-trip was obviously a huge relief to him. It also meant he could get some sleep tonight before he hit the road. I'd entertained the idea of going with him, but in the end, I decided that coming to get me at three o'clock in the morning would just make things more difficult for him. Besides, I was exhausted, and a good night's sleep was something I craved more than an early morning car ride to Dodge City.

We left the café a little after five thirty with four roast beef dinners and Dewey in tow. When we pulled into J.D.'s driveway, we ran into Inez Baumgartner backing out of the driveway. I jumped out of Amos's car and ran up to her window. She smiled at me and rolled it down.

"Why, Ivy," she said, "how nice of you to bring J.D. dinner. I left him some sliced ham and cheese for sandwiches. He should have enough to get by for a while."

Although Inez was at least twenty years older than her beautiful daughter, Emily, she could have been mistaken for her sister. During the vacations I'd spent in Winter Break with Aunt Bitty, I'd loved hanging around Emily's house so I could spend time around her mother. She was so different than mine. Inez could sew anything, was a fantastic cook, and her family absolutely adored her. Her late husband, Jake, used to light up whenever she came in the room. Inez had the unique ability to make a house a home. I'd watch her as she bustled around, always humming hymns. I learned to love several of the old hymns because of Aunt Bitty and Inez. They both loved the same songs. My favorites were "Softly and Tenderly," "The Old Rugged Cross," and "Blessed Assurance." Whenever I heard these songs, I was reminded of one rainy afternoon when Bitty and I visited at Emily's house. Inez played the piano while she and Bitty sang hymns. Emily and I sat on the floor and listened, scarfing down Inez's chocolate pecan cookies, fresh from the oven. It had been a perfect afternoon.

"I'm so glad to see you," I said, reaching through the car window to hug her while Amos juggled three Styrofoam containers of food. Dewey was holding on to his for all he was worth. "Thank you so much for offering to make my wedding dress. I really appreciate it."

Her large doe-brown eyes sparkled. "I was so excited to be asked. I've already found a basic pattern I think you will like."

I remembered the photo in Dela's folder. "Dela Shackelford gave me a picture of a wonderful dress. I'll make a copy and get it to you." I sighed. "With Dela's death and Ina Mae's accident, wedding plans have been put on the back burner."

She shook her head. "It hasn't been a good week in Winter Break, has it? A few people in town keep saying that disasters come in threes. They're waiting for something else terrible to happen. I think that's foolish, but it does make you wonder a bit."

"Hopefully, the next catastrophe will belong to Dela's killer," Amos said. "I think his time of reckoning is coming."

"My goodness, I hope so," Inez said. "You all better get inside before that food gets cold." She waved at Dewey, who was more focused on dinner than being neighborly. "Good to see you, Dewey. I've got some shopping to do. I'll see you tomorrow." She smiled at me. "Let me know when I can get a picture of that dress, Ivy. I'm so excited to see it."

I gave her my assurances and she pulled out. Amos, Dewey, and I tramped through the snow to J.D.'s front door. As we came up the driveway, I could see the steps in the back yard. I tried not to stare at them, but just a quick glimpse made me shiver with something besides the cold. J.D. answered the door after our first knock. I was grateful because my hands were freezing, even in gloves.

"Come on in," he said with a smile. "How nice of

you to bring dinner." He held the door open for us. The mat on the inside already held J.D.'s rubber boots. They were soon joined by three more sets. Boots were a part of everyone's wardrobe in Winter Break. With 90 percent of the winter spent wading through snow, they were almost a part of our bodies. Without them, cold feet and ruined shoes were the only possible result.

Although the house was small, it was neat and clean. A brown recliner sat near the fireplace. An old oak rocker was positioned near a forest green couch. A gorgeous patchwork quilt lay over its back. Against the wall was a curio cabinet. Its shelves were lined with framed pictures and statues of angels.

"Did Ina Mae collect angels?" I asked.

"Yes, she did," J.D. said. "She loved them."

"And did she make this quilt?" I couldn't take my eyes off of it. It had a cream-colored backing and each corner had five interlocking rings with flowers. The center of the quilt also had five colorful rings with a center of bright flowers. I'd never seen anything like it.

"Yes," J.D. said softly. "Ina Mae was really talented, but she never wanted to sell her work. She always gave away the things she made." His voice broke.

"I. . .I'm sorry, J.D.," I said. "Maybe I shouldn't have said anything."

"No, I like hearing about her. It's like she's still here." He pointed toward the back of the house. "Let's take this food into the kitchen before it gets cold."

Ina Mae's kitchen was also a reflection of her

creativity. Homemade oven mitts hung from kitchen drawer knobs, and patchwork curtains framed the windows. It was a homey, cozy kitchen, obviously owned by someone who liked to spend time there. J. D. moved a suitcase off the table and put in on the floor near the back door.

"I'm going to Liberal tomorrow," he said, pointing at the suitcase. "Elmer is taking Ina Mae there for the funeral. I hope you can all come. I hate to make it inconvenient for our friends in Winter Break, but except for her mother, all of Ina Mae's family lives in Liberal."

"Will her mother be able to attend the funeral?" Dewey asked.

"Unfortunately, no. She's very ill. To be honest, no one has told her about Ina Mae. They don't think she'll last much longer, and we don't have the heart to cause her that kind of pain. Of course, she's been in and out of reality for so long I doubt she'll even realize Ina Mae hasn't come to see her."

"That's a shame." I could understand the decision not to tell her about her daughter's death, but somehow it seemed worse for the old woman to think she'd been deserted. I hoped J.D. was right and she wouldn't be aware of Ina Mae's absence.

We sat down at the table and opened our containers. The aroma of Ruby's incredible roast beef wafted through the room. J.D. got us silverware and napkins. Then he took a pitcher of iced tea out of the refrigerator and filled glasses he set on the table.

"Anything else?" he asked, looking back and forth at each of us.

"Can't think of a thing," Dewey said, "except grace. Do you mind if I pray?"

J.D. smiled. "I'd be honored."

Dewey blessed the food and prayed that God would comfort J.D. and help him through the next few days. He also asked the Lord to console Barney and bring Dela's killer to justice. We all added our "amens" and started shoveling food into our mouths like we hadn't eaten in days. That just kind of happened with Ruby and Bert's food. Dewey grumbled a little because his roast beef was sans gravy, and instead of a potato, he had fresh green beans and a piece of whole grain bread, but all in all, he was satisfied.

We talked some about Ina Mae's service. J.D. wasn't sure when the funeral would be held. "My guess is Monday or Tuesday," he said. "Taking her to the mortuary on Saturday means we'll have to wait a bit before she's ready. I'll call you and let you know as soon as I know something definite."

"Will you come right back?" Amos asked.

J.D. shook his head, his eyes full of sorrow. "I'll probably stay there awhile. I think it will help to have Ina Mae's family around, and of course, we have old, dear friends there." He smiled at us. "Not that you're not good friends."

I reached over and grabbed his hand. "We all

understand. You need to do whatever helps you. But we're here for you if you need us."

His eyes filled up with tears which he wiped away on his sleeve. "Thank you. You have no idea what that means to me."

We chatted for a while longer about some of the goings on in Winter Break. I checked my watch and saw that it was getting late. "I hate to break this up, but Amos has to drive to Dodge City around three o'clock in the morning to pick my mother up at the train station. He needs his beauty sleep."

"Before you go," J.D. said, looking at me, "I want to give you something for your wedding. Something from Ina Mae." He pointed toward the living room. "Would you like to have that quilt? I know Ina Mae would be blessed to know it went to you. It's the way she was."

I started to protest but realized that if I refused, it might hurt his feelings. "I'd love it, J.D.," I said. "It's the most beautiful quilt I've ever seen."

"I'll get a plastic bag for it before you leave. I'm so happy you like it. Maybe you'll remember her when you see it."

"Goodness," Amos said. "Barney gave you some of Dela's jewelry, now J.D.'s giving you Ina Mae's quilt."

J.D. picked up our food containers and carried them to the trash can. "Barney gave you some of Dela's jewelry? That's was really nice of him. I'm sure Dela would be pleased."

"Actually, she'd already picked it out for me. She wanted me to wear it at my wedding." I pulled the jewelry box out of my purse. Dewey hadn't had a chance to see it either.

"Why, Ivy, those are absolutely beautiful," Dewey said when I opened the box. "Dela was right. You definitely should wear them at your wedding."

"That's exactly what I intend to do. Dela thought they would go with my hair."

Amos smiled. "She was right."

I popped the lid shut. "I think she was wearing an emerald necklace with matching earrings the night she. . ." I couldn't finish.

J.D. came up behind me and patted my shoulder. "Ivy, I'm not a jewelry expert, but that set was designed a lot differently than this one and it was set in gold, not silver. Please don't let the fact that the stones are the same color ruin Dela's gift to you. They're not connected."

I fought back tears. "You're right. Thanks, J.D. Guess I'm feeling a little emotional tonight." I put the box back in my purse. "The important thing is that Dela's gift was from the heart. They could all be made out of plastic and it wouldn't make any difference."

Amos grunted. "So I could have given you an engagement ring from a Cracker Jack's box and it would have meant as much to you as what you're wearing? I wish you'd told me that *before* I spent all that money."

"Oh hush," I said brusquely. "Spending money

on someone you love is good for the soul. I was only helping you."

"Uh-oh," Dewey said with a grin. "That womanly reasoning only gets worse as time goes on. You might as well hand over your wallet and be done with it."

"You watch out, old man," I said, laughing. "You're sleeping in my house tonight, you know. You better keep one eye open."

J.D. put Ina Mae's quilt in a bag and handed it to me as we left. I hugged him. "Thank you so much, and let us know about the service. I'm sure we'll be there."

J.D. stood in the doorway waving as we left. He looked so forlorn and alone, I almost made Amos drive back, but I couldn't think of anything else we could do for him but pray. We got home around seven o'clock. I made Amos a pot of coffee while Dewey watched TV in the living room.

"Thanks for picking my mother up," I said. "Sorry I'm punking out on you. I've got to get some sleep. I'm exhausted, and my mother's going to take all the energy I have. At least I won't have to worry about the wedding. She'll have things whipped into shape in no time."

Amos chuckled. "I don't doubt that."

I set a cup of hot coffee in front of him and made myself a cup of caffeine-free raspberry tea. I didn't want anything keeping me awake tonight. "Anything new on your bank robber?"

Amos sighed deeply. "Absolutely nothing. I'm

beginning to wonder if we'll ever catch him. But I don't want to talk about him now. Let's discuss our visits today. I've been going over several different scenarios in my mind." He scooted his stool up closer to the counter and stared into his cup. "Most of the time when a spouse is murdered, the husband or the wife is guilty. Therefore, I can't rule out Barney. Statistically, he's the number-one suspect. I know it seems as if he really loved Dela, but playing the bereaved partner has certainly been done before. I'd like to find out if she really was having an affair. That would make things a lot clearer."

"I'm not convinced she was," I said doubtfully. "It's entirely possible that the man she was seen with in Dodge City was J.D. But we can't be sure about that. There may be someone else involved who isn't even on our radar screen."

"That's true. And then I have to look at Ina Mae. She sure was carrying some heavy burden—something she felt she needed prayer for. Maybe she followed Dela that night to your house and attacked her. Whoever killed her didn't plan it ahead of time. A fight over J. D. fits the bill exactly."

"And J.D. can't give her an alibi. She could have left the house that night."

"And Hope isn't out of the picture. So far, she has the clearest motive." He rubbed his hands across his face. "You know what bothers me? Why didn't Dela tell Barney about that bracelet? Was it really because he told her not to buy so much jewelry? This whole bracelet business. I think it might be important."

"Yes, it could be, but I still don't think Hope is a killer."

Amos reached over and stroked my hair. "My beautiful Ivy, you don't think anyone is capable of murder."

"I'm afraid that's not true anymore," I said, taking his hand in mine. "I've learned people are capable of great evil, but it's hard to spot them because they never see themselves as villains. In some twisted way, they believe they're victims trying to right some terrible wrong done to them."

"You're right. It doesn't matter what crime someone's committed, they always seem to have an excuse. I guess the first step toward murder is convincing yourself you have a valid reason to eradicate a human being who has interfered in your life. It's the worst kind of selfishness."

I sighed. "This is getting too deep for me and my tired brain."

Amos stood up. "I'm going home to get some sleep before driving to Dodge City." He leaned over and kissed me. "And God bless you for coming up with this new plan. If I had to drive to Wichita tonight, I don't know what I'd do." He walked over to the French doors in the dining room. "What's going on with your visitor?"

"I don't know. I gave him your eggs this morning.

Is he out there?"

"I can't tell, but I don't see him." He pushed the door open and stepped outside. He came back a moment later. "Sorry, honey," he said. "The eggs are still there and so is the water. Either he didn't come back today or he doesn't like eggs."

I felt my emotions well up, but I didn't want to cry in front of Amos because he'd already warned me about getting attached to the dog. Truth was, I was in desperate need of a happy ending.

"Oh, well," I said as casually as possible. "I'll put out something else before I go to bed. It's probably a critique of your cooking."

"Oh, thanks." He wrapped his arms around me. "I'll see you in the morning. I'm looking forward to spending some time with your mother. She's a super lady."

"Yes, she is. I'm glad she's coming, too. Dewey can finally go home tomorrow."

Amos glanced toward Dewey, who was watching one of the cable news channels. "I'm not so sure he'll be happy to leave," he whispered. "I think he likes it here."

"I love having him here. Maybe we can adopt him and he can live with us after we're married."

He wrinkled his nose like he was considering it. "Hmmm. Well, I was thinking more toward someone younger, but maybe we could make do with Dewey."

I bopped him on the head, and he kissed me again.

"I love you, you know," he said softly into my ear.

"I know. I'm fond of you, too."

He laughed and let me go. "I better quit while I'm behind." He headed for the front door. "See you tomorrow, Dewey," he said as he walked past the couch.

"'Night, Amos."

Before Amos closed the door, he blew me a kiss. I went back to the kitchen and finished my tea. Then I went outside to check on the dog. Just as Amos had said, the eggs were still there. I brought both the bowls inside and cleaned them out. I went through my refrigerator, but I couldn't find anything I thought a dog would like. I checked the pantry and found some cans of corned beef hash. I dumped the contents of two of them into the food bowl, filled the other one with water, and carried them outside. After I put the bowls in the toolshed, I stared out into the dark, hoping to see the dog. The temperature was really dropping. I would have loved to set up a small heater in the shed, but it was too dangerous. Since the shed backed up next to the house, I hoped it would help to provide a little warmth.

By the time I got back inside the house, Dewey had turned off the TV. "Think I'll head upstairs to bed," he said. "I'm not real tired, but I have some reading I want to do. Burrowing under the covers with a book sounds like the perfect evening."

"It does sound nice, but I don't think I'd make it

past the first page. I'm heading up in a few minutes." I went over to my old friend and gave him a big hug. He hugged me back.

"Good night, sweetheart," he said. "You know, Ivy, I couldn't love you more if you were my own child."

"I know that," I answered, blinking back tears. "You're as much family as anyone in my life."

He let his arms drop and turned to go upstairs. "Sometimes I miss your aunt Bitty so much I can hardly stand it," he said in a quiet voice. "And then sometimes, like right now, I could swear she was still here." He smiled at me, but I knew he was seeing Bitty. And it was okay with me. With that, he walked carefully up the stairs, holding tightly to the handrail. For the first time, I realized how much slower he was moving these days. Dewey was getting older, and I couldn't imagine my life without him. Someday he would be gone. I just hoped that day was a long time coming.

I went back to the kitchen and made another cup of tea, toasted an English muffin, and slathered it with butter and huckleberry jelly. All I wanted to do was fall into bed, but for some reason I was reluctant to go upstairs. I felt like there was something I'd forgotten or something I was supposed to do. I sat down at the dining room table and stared out into the night. The only illumination came from the lights near the lake. Cecil had strung them years ago for night skating. Amos frequently had to replace bulbs. He wanted the city to install some decorative light poles around the lake. So far, it hadn't been approved.

My foot hit something and I looked down. My purse was lying on the floor where I'd dropped it when we came in. I picked it up and set it on the table. Remembering the jewelry box, I reached into my purse and took it out. When I opened it, I was captivated again by how beautiful the pieces were. Green really was my best color.

Once again, the feeling that there was something I was missing flitted through my brain. "What is it?" I whispered. "What am I not seeing?" I suddenly remembered something Aunt Bitty said once about worrying. Truth was, she had several admonitions when it came to worry. She believed faith and worry were absolute opposites. "Worrying never solved a single problem, Ivy. Casting your care on the Lord gives Him a chance to work things out." I took a deep breath and tried to relax a little.

When I took a bite of my muffin, a thought jumped into my mind. Something that had been said that didn't make sense—until I began to put it with all the other strange pieces of the deadly riddle Amos and I had been working on.

That "Sherlock Holmes moment" Amos hoped for had finally arrived, but there were still a few odd puzzle pieces that didn't seem to fit. Unless I could match them into all the remaining blank spaces, and create a comprehensible final picture, a murderer was going to go free.

Sitting in the dark waiting to confront a killer is an interesting experience. On one hand, you feel triumphant because you're getting ready to catch someone who's committed a truly evil deed. On the other hand, you wonder just how many brain cells you could possibly have if you're willing to put yourself within range of the person who's committed a truly evil deed. These thoughts had been running through my mind for a little over an hour. Of course it could have been fifteen minutes. . .or two hours. I had no idea. It's hard to see your watch in the dark. I was getting extremely uncomfortable seated on an old step stool Cecil and Marion had left in the basement when they moved. It definitely had been made for feet—not bottoms.

Even though I'd been expecting it for quite some time, when I heard the door to the basement open and steps coming near me, my heart felt as if it would jump right out of my chest. From my vantage point, I could see the dark shape of the killer pass by me. A flashlight came on and swept over the shelves that held Bubba Weber's honey and my precious huckleberry jelly. I waited until gloved hands began to take the jars from the shelves and set them on top of my washer and dryer. Then I flipped on the light switch next to me.

"You're not going to get away with it, you know,"

I said, trying to keep my voice from shaking. "I know what you did."

My intruder quickly swung around, eyes wide with shock. "What? What are you doing down here?"

"Well, I live here. I'm pretty sure you're the person who doesn't belong."

"I. . .I was worried about you. With Amos gone and. . ."

I would have laughed if I wasn't so nervous. "You thought you'd break into my house, check out how much huckleberry jelly I had, and somehow that would keep me safe?"

The realization that there was no way to explain the situation seemed to finally dawn on him. "No. I guess I don't expect you to believe that." He sighed and leaned against my washing machine, his eyes never leaving my face. His original look of surprise had been replaced with amusement. "Okay, I'll bite. Tell me what you think I did, Ivy."

I cleared my throat. Nerves were making it hard for me to catch my breath. My obvious discomfort seemed to add to his pleasure. "If you don't mind, I'd rather start with what tipped me off. What it was that finally helped me to see that you were the only person who could have killed Dela."

"I thought I covered myself pretty well. I'd be interested to hear what gave me away."

I tried to wiggle into a more comfortable position on the step stool. Instead of stabilizing myself, I was afraid I detected a slight shift in the old, rather rotten wood. I purposely leaned against the wall. Having my stool collapse beneath me would certainly reduce the drama of the moment. This was what mystery writers call the *denouement*—the moment when all the clues are revealed. And I didn't want to spend it in a heap on the floor. Still feeling rather vulnerable, I gave him my best Sherlock Holmes look. "It was the jewelry that Dela gave me. You compared it to the jewelry she was wearing when she died. Both sets had green stones."

"So?" J.D. said, looking puzzled. "I was right about that."

"Yes, you were. But how would you know what color her jewelry was? You came in late to the city council meeting, and you and Ina Mae were almost thirty feet away from us. Dela left when we did. You never got close enough to see the color of her accessories."

J.D. laughed. "That's it? That's what revealed me as the killer?" He shook his head. "I ran into her earlier in the day, before I left town. That's when I saw what she was wearing."

"Just my point. You see, Dela was wearing *red* and gold jewelry until right before the meeting when she changed to *green* and gold. You know as well as I do that Dela would sometimes switch her accessories several times a day. Yet not only did you know she was wearing green jewelry, you even knew they were set in gold, not silver like mine. You corrected me when I compared my jewelry to what she was wearing when she died. The only way you could have known that was if you saw her sometime after the city council meeting. Since she went straight to my house, you had to see her there—when you killed her."

He raised one eyebrow and considered this. "Okay. I'll give you that point. Go on."

"After realizing it was you, all kinds of other things fell into place. For one thing, you are the only person who could have called in all those tips. Except the one that Bertha Pennypacker phoned in."

"Bertha Pennypacker? What kind of tip would she have?"

"Never mind, it's not important. What *is* important is that you were the only one who knew about the bracelet. It wasn't hard to figure out that Dela also told you about the trouble with Barney. You told me that you and Dela spent a lot of time together while you were selling their house. It stands to reason that Dela told you *why* they had to move."

"Wait a minute." J.D. scratched his chin for a moment. "Barney could have phoned in those tips. He had all the same information."

"No. He didn't know anything about the bracelet. He never even knew Dela had it."

J.D. shifted his weight and crossed his arms. "How do you know that?"

"Easy. He told us. The bracelet must have been one of the pieces she kept secret. And it was pretty easy to figure out why you placed those phone calls. You were trying to misdirect the authorities. To keep them busy looking somewhere else. If they were investigating Barney or Hope, or even Ina Mae, it would give you time. You were trying to create as many red herrings as possible in an attempt to keep yourself off the radar screen."

"What about Hope? She could have done it."

I shook my head. "No. She was just an innocent bystander. Her story was absolutely true. Dela did feel badly about buying the bracelet for so little. She returned it. Dela must have told you she was going to do it."

A slow smile spread across his face, but his eyes were dead and cold. They reminded me of the pictures I'd seen of sharks. There was no remorse, no fear, only icy, clear calculation. I wondered if he was weighing his options about me. "She told me Sunday afternoon. Then on my way out of town on Tuesday, I saw her entering the library. It wasn't hard to figure out what she was up to."

"You lied when you said the person who wanted the bracelet was threatening Dela. You wanted me to think that Hope might have killed her for the bracelet."

He straightened up but made no move toward me. I was watching him, waiting for him to make a threatening gesture. But to him, this was a game, and he was too engrossed in it to stop it now. And too curious to know how I had tracked his moves.

"So far I'm impressed," he said, still smiling. "But

there's more, isn't there? I mean—"

"You mean why are we here?"

"Exactly."

"Two reasons." There was definite movement from beneath me. "I've got to stand up. I've been sitting here too long. Do you mind?"

He gave me a quick bow. "Be my guest."

I slowly lowered myself from the stool, being careful to stay as far away from him as possible. I took a couple of steps to the left of my creaky, wooden nemesis and leaned against the wall. The circulation was returning to my extremities, but I was still well out of his reach. Of course if he moved quickly. . .

"That's close enough," he snapped. "Get to it, please. I have someplace I have to be. I can't give you much more of my time."

Maybe he wasn't as absorbed in our game as I thought. I felt a chill run through me. But since it was cold in the basement, it was hard to tell if my reaction was from fear or temperature. "Before we talk about why we're both shivering in my basement, I want to know something."

Again, he bowed with a flourish. "Ask away. It seems we have no secrets anymore."

"Did you intend to kill Dela when you met her at my house?"

For the first time, I saw a hint of remorse on his face. He hung his head slightly and lost some of the swagger he'd been exhibiting. "No. I followed her after the meeting. When she pulled into your driveway, I parked behind her and got out. I told her I wanted to talk to her and she let me get into her car. I asked her to. . .well, you seem to know what I asked her. Instead of trusting me, she got suspicious. I ended up telling her the truth. I pleaded with her to come away with me—to share everything I had. But she wouldn't listen. She told me she loved that Pillsbury Doughboy of a husband of hers, and she threatened to turn me in. We struggled and her purse hit the floor. Those stupid chopsticks fell out. Before I knew it, I'd grabbed one and I—I stabbed her." His eyes sought mine. "I didn't mean to hurt her. I loved her." Then his expression hardened again. "But she gave me no choice. It was her own fault. There wasn't anything else I could do."

"Nothing else you could do?" I said incredulously. "You could have let her live. You could have walked away." He took a step closer to me. It was casual but definite. I forced myself not to react. I needed more time.

"I couldn't walk away. If you truly know everything—you must understand why. Let's hear what you've figured out. I want to know if you're as smart as you think you are."

Actually, right at that moment I wasn't feeling too intelligent, but our game hadn't been played out yet. I had a few more moves to make. "Okay. I have no idea when you decided to start robbing banks. My guess is that as you handled properties in lots of rural communities, you began to see how unprotected some of the small banks were. It was easy for you to learn when big deposits were being made. If you couldn't get the information from your client, a few lunches in the local cafés gave you everything you needed."

He laughed. "Good job. You *are* sharp. Go on."

I cleared my throat again. I wasn't sure whether it was the dust in the basement or nerves, but my throat felt scratchy. "I suspect you told me the truth about Ina Mae. She really was suspicious of you. I'm pretty sure she had good reason to be, even though you weren't having an affair with Dela. She probably *was* going through your things, looking for evidence that you were cheating. Because of that, I doubt that you had any decent hiding places for your booty. But then you had an idea. A safe place that no one else knew about."

"Now, wait a minute," J.D. said in a rather irritated tone. "I can see how you made all your other assumptions, but there is no way you could have known about the hiding place. I've checked regularly to make sure no one but me has moved things. You're going to have to explain this one."

Even though I was somewhat fearful for my safety, I couldn't suppress a slight smile. "It was really Miss Skiffins who gave it away."

He frowned. "Your cat? I don't get it."

"Well, Miss Skiffins and huckleberry jelly." J.D.'s puzzled expression told me he still hadn't put it together. "First of all, I found a piece of the jar you broke while you were down here hiding the money. At the time, I didn't think anything about it. I figured Amos broke the jar and didn't tell me. But then, Miss Skiffins acted so strangely around your boots. Earlier this evening, when I was trying to piece all of this together, I was eating an English muffin with huckleberry jelly. And I realized that she was attracted to your boots because you had them on when you broke the jar of jelly. Even though you thought you'd cleaned up the mess, you missed one piece of the jar, and you really didn't clean your boots off very well. You see, Miss Skiffins is crazy about huckleberry jelly. She was trying to lick it off your boots."

Now he really did look confused. "But I walked through the snow. There shouldn't have been any jelly left on my boots."

"You don't know much about jelly, do you? It's sticky and hard to clean off. Maybe if it had been warmer in Winter Break and you'd been walking in wet, sloppy snow, you'd have had a chance. But since our temperatures haven't risen above freezing since your visit to my basement, your boots retained enough jelly to attract my cat."

He shook his head and he took one more step toward me. "Anything else?"

"Yes. You started hiding the money in my basement when the house was still empty. Of course you had a key. You were the real estate agent handling the property. You still have a key to my front door.

When Amos bought the house, you probably weren't too worried. The house can't be seen from the road. You could come here anytime I wasn't here, let yourself in, and hide more money."

"Since we don't have much time left," he interjected, "why don't you let me finish tying up all the loose ends?"

"Be my guest."

"Thank you." His gaze swept around the room, then rested on the shelves against the wall. "I'd already been working on a plan to rob several banks, hide the money, then leave town and start a new life. You see, I was tired of Ina Mae, tired of being married, and yes, there were other women. One in particular. She doesn't live in Winter Break and she has no idea I'm married. We have plans to move to somewhere warm. Somewhere safe where no one will ever find me. But I was having problems figuring out where to hide what you call my 'booty.' Then one day I was on the phone with Cecil Biddle, and he was telling me about how he had redone the old kitchen in this house. How it used to actually be part of what's now your dining room. He just happened to mention the old dumbwaiter behind the shelves in the basement. It was the perfect place. Since all the parts were finally in place, I put my plan in action. But two things happened I didn't count on."

"Me and Dela."

"Kind of. You and your wedding. That was what changed everything."

I stared at him and shook my head. "You know now that I wouldn't have had that tapestry taken down, don't you? You killed Dela for no reason whatsoever."

He shrugged and stared at the floor. "I gave her a chance. I knew if you found the other door to the dumbwaiter behind the tapestry, you would have discovered my money. I told Dela all she had to do was to tell you to leave the tapestry up and wait for me to get the money from the last bank. Then we could leave this one-horse town together. We could have been happy."

"What about your girlfriend?"

"I really would have taken Dela instead. She was the most intriguing woman I ever met."

"Unfortunately for you, she was not only in love with her husband, she was too ethical to live on stolen money."

J.D. sighed. "This has been very interesting, but I really have to get going."

"Just two more things I want to clear up." I'd been keeping my eyes on his body language. He was getting restless. I had one final card to play, but I wanted to hold it until the very last moment. I could see that it was coming quickly. "Why are you still here? Why haven't you left town? Hanging around so you could get caught doesn't make much sense."

He eyes narrowed and he glared at me. "I couldn't possibly have taken off right after Dela was killed. It would have looked too suspicious. Besides, I had one more bank to hit to bring me to my goal of half a million dollars."

"But if you'd just taken what you already had and left Winter Break, Dela would still be alive. You could have gotten the money out before anyone took down the tapestry. No one would have ever suspected you."

He frowned at me like I'd lost my mind. "I couldn't take the chance that Dela wasn't going to start fooling around with the tapestry Tuesday night. Even if she hadn't, leaving early wasn't in my plan. I'd worked too hard to set everything up. I had one more bank, and I had no intention of letting anything keep me from getting everything I was entitled to. This really wasn't my fault, you know," he said, glowering at me. "If you'd been capable of planning your own wedding, everything would have turned out fine."

It was obvious to me that J.D. was so locked up in chains of evil that the idea of not fulfilling his selfish goals had never occurred to him. "That brings me to one last question." For the first time since we'd begun our strange exchange, my emotions got the better of me, and I couldn't stop the tears that formed in my eyes. "Why did you have to kill Ina Mae?"

He grinned. "I had everything I needed except a way out of town. Ina Mae gave me the perfect excuse." He stuck out his bottom lip and tried to look sad. "I have to bury my wife, and because of my incredible grief, I'm going away for a while." His forced melancholy expression disappeared and his lips parted in a big grin. "No one would ever think to follow me. You know, Ina Mae really was taking food to the dogs. A small push from me was all it took on those slippery stairs. Thank goodness the fall killed her. Of course, I would have been more than willing to finish the job if it had been necessary, but it wasn't. Her 'accident' solved everything. Then I drove over here, put my car in a ditch, and used you for my alibi. It seemed like the perfect solution. It also gave me a chance to make sure the tapestry was still where it should be."

"And now you're back to pick up your money."

He grinned. "I needed to get it before I left town, and you let me know when your boyfriend would be gone. With just you and Dewey in the house and Amos too far away to do anything to stop me. . ."

"You figured you had the perfect setup."

"That's it." He reached into his pocket and pulled out a gun. "Too bad you decided to play Miss Detective. I'm afraid your snooping is going to end very badly. I'll shoot you if I have to, but I don't think it will be necessary. Unfortunately, I'm afraid you're about to have an accident yourself. Those stairs don't look very safe, do they? I think you came down here to get something and you slipped and fell."

"Another murder, J.D.?" I asked.

For just a moment, the look in his eyes changed and I saw a trace of vulnerability. "I didn't start out with the intention of hurting anyone. I wouldn't have shot the guy in Chevron, but he forced my hand. And I didn't want to kill Dela." He took a deep, ragged breath. "The weird thing is that each time it gets easier. I don't really understand why. But it does." The hardness came back into his face.

"The more you give to the devil, the more he owns you," I said softly. "He's got a stronghold on you now. I pray someday you'll kick him out and give yourself to God. Even with everything you've done, He'll still forgive you and love you."

This time he threw his head back and laughed heartily. But he who had the last laugh. . .well, you know. It was time for the last play of this game. I raised my voice. "Take nothing on its looks; take everything on evidence. There's no better rule."

Before J.D. had the chance to wipe the puzzled look from his face, a voice came from behind him. "Put the gun down, J.D. There's nowhere to go and no way out of here." J.D. swung around to see Amos, who had stepped around the corner and had his gun pointed right at his chest. As he lifted his gun around toward the man I loved, I finally moved from my spot. A jar of huckleberry jelly is good for many things. Conking a killer on the head wouldn't have normally been on my list, but it did the job. He didn't lose consciousness, but he dropped his gun. That was good enough for Amos.

"I thought I told you to stay put, little lady," Sheriff Hitchens said harshly. "I had it covered." He stepped up behind Amos, his gun also drawn.

"Sorry, Sheriff," I said, "but I couldn't take a chance."

While Amos put cuffs on J.D., the sheriff yelled up the stairs for the other deputies who were waiting. "Bag that gun," he barked at one of them. "I'm pretty sure it will match the bullet we have from the robbery in Chevron." He got up in J.D.'s face, which had gone completely ashen. "We gotcha good, son," he droned in his deep, bullfrog voice. "You not only confessed to all those bank robberies, we got you on assault and two counts of murder. You're goin' away for a long, long time."

With that, the sheriff turned and smiled at me. I was shaking so hard, I wasn't certain I was capable of staying upright. Had I really just attacked a cold-blooded killer with a jelly jar?

"You can thank this young woman for puttin' you away," he continued. "After she figured out you were the guy we were lookin' for, she called us. And just so you know, we took that bank money out of here before you ever arrived."

J.D. was speechless. He looked sicker than any human being I'd ever seen in my life. The sheriff handed him to one of the deputies who stood near us. "Put him in the car and stay with him. We're not lettin' this yahoo get away." He put his face near J.D.'s and glowered at him. "And Deputy Biggins, if Mr. Feldhammer here so much as moves an eyebrow, shoot him, will you?"

J.D.'s eyes widened and he went limp. As the deputy pushed him up the stairs he looked completely defeated. And I guess he was.

Sheriff Hitchens stuck his hand out and I took it. "Little lady, I guess you really are Sherlock Holmes, Junior. Sorry I ever doubted you. Our friend here could have been layin' on a beach in Acapulco before we ever figured this one out. You did a good job. If you're ever interested in working for the Sheriff's Department. . ."

I grinned at him. "After tonight, Sheriff, I'm ready to exchange my cape and magnifying glass for a wedding dress and a quiet life in Winter Break. I'm afraid there will only be one deputy sheriff in this family."

"I understand." He smiled and squeezed my hand. Then he left, following his deputies upstairs and, thankfully, out of my house.

Amos grabbed me and squeezed me so hard I yelped. After a long hug and an even longer kiss, he pulled back and gazed into my eyes. "That was a harebrained idea, Ivy. Luring J.D. down here and getting him to confess to everything."

"It was the only way we could be sure to put him away for good, Amos," I said. "You know that. All we had was circumstantial evidence. Except for the bullet in his gun. But we needed to get him for the murders, not just the bank robberies. We all discussed it before we made the decision. Even Sheriff Hitchens agreed it was a good idea."

"But when he took out that gun. . .what if he'd shot you before we had a chance to get to you?" Amos's eyes were wet. I reached up and wiped a tear from the corner of one of his beautiful eyes.

"But he didn't. And now we know that Dela and Ina Mae's killer will pay for what he did. It was all worth it."

"Let's not argue about it anymore," he said. "I'm freezing. We need to go upstairs and warm up a little." He looked at his watch. "Deputy Winslow should be back with your mother around seven thirty or eight. You can still get a little sleep before she arrives."

"A little sleep? That's where you're wrong, bucko. I'm going to sleep until I can't sleep anymore. You tell my mother to make herself comfortable. I'll see her when I see her."

His face turned pale. "You're going to make me explain to her that you put yourself in danger to solve another murder? That should go over well. And don't call me bucko."

I kissed him. "And good luck to you. Hope the fireworks have died down by the time I wake up."

I started to leave but he grabbed me once again. "And will I also have to explain the cue you made us use so we'd know when to arrest J.D.?"

"You mean, 'Take nothing on its looks; take everything on evidence. There's no better rule'?"

He nodded. "We didn't have much time to set things up, but don't you think we could have come up with something better than that?"

"Like what?" I asked, laughing. "Like 'Hey, Amos, please get in here before he kills me'? I think that might have taken away the element of surprise."

Amos smiled and shook his head. "I was standing back there repeating that stupid phrase over and over so I'd recognize it when you said it."

"Why, Amos, I thought you told me you'd read all the classics. I'm surprised you didn't recognize a quote from *Great Expectations.*"

"Charles Dickens. For crying out loud."

"Well, I think it was a perfect choice. In honor of Miss Skiffins. She's the real hero of this story, you know."

"Speaking of Miss Skiffins, let's buy her a whole fish of her own. She deserves it."

I took his hand. "That's a wonderful idea." I reached over and put my other hand on the light switch. But first I took a long look around at the room. "You know, we really should do something with this old basement. It deserves to be updated."

"I agree. But let's get married first and leave the redecorating for later, okay?"

"You've got a deal." I switched off the light and we went upstairs. As I closed the door to the basement, I noticed that it was terribly cold as we walked into the kitchen. A look toward the dining room told the story. One of the officers had left the French door to the deck open.

"Please tell me you put Miss Skiffins up before the sheriff got here," Amos said.

The whole evening had been so confusing, for a moment I couldn't remember. "Yes. . .yes, I did. I put her in the bathroom down the hall."

Amos hurried down toward the bathroom door. "It's open," he said.

We both began calling the tiny calico cat. Of course, even under the best circumstances cats will treat anyone who beckons them with utter and complete disregard, but cat owners never give up. I finally pulled a can of cat food out of the pantry and put it under the electric can opener. This always produced an immediate reaction. But no cat came running around the corner.

Amos had gone upstairs to check for her, but when he reached the bottom of the stairs, I knew he hadn't found her. "Oh, Amos," I said. "She's gotten out. We've got to go look for her. It's way below freezing out there."

Without another word, we bundled up and stepped out into the cold, dark morning. It was snowing again, making it even harder to see. We turned on all the back lights and the lights around the lake. Amos and I both had flashlights. We began calling Miss Skiffins. The idea of her outside in these conditions terrified me. She was so little. . . *Trust God, child.* Aunt Bitty's admonition welled up from inside of me. How many times had she encouraged me to walk in faith? *Perfect love casts out fear, Ivy. Don't be full of fear, be full of faith.* "Easy for you to say, Bitty," I said under my breath. "You're dead." But I knew she was right. I grabbed Amos's hand and prayed, "God, please help us find Miss Skiffins. You know how much we love her. She needs You now and so do we."

"Amen," Amos said. We searched the deck and were just getting ready to go out into the yard when Amos took hold of my arm and stopped me.

"What's that?" he asked.

There was something moving through the yard, coming toward us. But it was too big to be Miss Skiffins. Amos swung his flashlight toward it and it stopped.

"Oh no!" I cried. It was the dog, and he had something in his mouth. As he started to come closer, I started to say something, but Amos shushed me.

"Ivy, just be quiet," he whispered. "Don't say a word. I mean it."

It wasn't hard to follow his advice. I was heartbroken. Tears were running down my face. I'd befriended this dog and he'd killed Miss Skiffins. It was all my fault. The dog kept advancing, slowly, carefully. Keeping his eyes focused on us.

"Don't move, Ivy," Amos said softly. "Stay perfectly still."

I looked up at him. Amos didn't look very upset. In fact, there was a small smile on his face. Was it possible? Could she still be alive? I turned to watch the collie walk deliberately up the stairs to the deck. Gradually, one paw in front of the other, he advanced until he was only a few feet away from us. He lowered his mouth and gingerly released a rather offended calico cat that ran straight to us, completely unharmed. She delivered one hiss of complaint to the dog before allowing me to scoop her up into my arms.

"Ivy," Amos said softly, "take Miss Skiffins inside and for crying out loud, close all the doors. I'm staying out here for a while."

I started to say something, but he shushed me. I was getting a little tired of being told to be quiet, but I was so grateful to have Miss Skiffins back and unharmed, I didn't care. I carefully backed up toward the house and went inside. After feeding Miss Skiffins, hugging her until she swatted at me, and finally letting her curl up on the sofa next to the fire, I sat down at the table next to the French doors and watched Amos. He was sitting on the deck, only a few feet away from the dog. He had to be almost frozen, but he didn't move. And surprisingly enough, neither did the dog. I could see Amos's lips moving, so I knew he was talking to the small collie. And the dog was watching him—with interest. Finally, after about thirty minutes of encouragement, the dog moved closer to Amos. And within another few minutes, Amos was petting him and the dog was doing something I'd never seen him do before. He was wagging his tail. And then the most incredible thing happened. Amos got up and walked to the door. He opened it and turned to look at the dog who stood there, staring back and forth between Amos and me. And then he trotted inside my house. Amos went into the kitchen and took two bowls from the shelves. He put water in one and opened a can of beef stew from the pantry and plopped it into the other bowl. "We're going to have to get some actual dog food," he said to me with a smile. "We can't keep feeding Pal people food."

"Pal?"

Amos came up next to me. "I think his name is Pal. It fits him."

I had to agree. It did fit. *Nothing so broken that God can't mend it.* Those words kept going through my mind. They were true. With God, nothing at all was impossible.

While we waited for Pal to finish eating, we stood next to the windows and watched the snow fall. Amos wrapped his arms around my waist and nuzzled my neck. After a few minutes of watching the fat, white flakes drift down from the sky, I checked the lock on the door and turned around to walk Amos to the front door. I happened to glance toward the tapestry. Then I stopped cold and leaned in closer, looking at it carefully. How could there be something in this painting I'd never noticed before?

"Amos," I said slowly. "What is this? Do you see what I see?"

My great aunt Bitty still sat on the bench by the lake, Emily Baumgartner next to her, and she was still waving to me, but for the first time I noticed the dog lying by her feet. A black-and-white border collie.

"I don't get it," Amos said. "I've looked at this thing a hundred times. Why didn't I ever see. . ."

I leaned over and kissed him before he could say anything else. “Sometimes you just accept miracles, Amos,” I whispered. “You don’t question them.”

13

Hard to believe it's all over."

Amos and I were watching snowflakes drift lazily to the ground. The lights on Lake Winter Break were twinkling and the house was still decorated for the reception. All our guests had left, and we were finally alone.

"It was a perfect wedding," Amos said, scooting his chair next to mine and putting his arm around me. He'd changed out of his tux and had on jeans and a sweater. I'd taken off my wedding dress and put on my green jumper. "You looked like an angel coming down the aisle. I don't believe I've ever seen anything so beautiful in all my life." He leaned over and kissed me. It was long, lingering, and delicious.

When he finally pulled away, I smiled at him. "Even with our choice of ring bearer?"

Amos chuckled and looked down at Pal sleeping peacefully at our feet. Miss Skiffins was snuggled up next to him like some kind of oddly shaped puppy. "*Especially* with our choice of ring bearer. He did a wonderful job."

He really had been cute in his little doggy tux, prancing proudly down the aisle with our rings strapped to his back. He'd brought them straight to us, then sat absolutely still while Amos removed the pillow from his back. When my dad snapped his fingers, Pal had taken his place of honor on the front row, next to my proud parents. He'd done a much better job than Lulu-belle the pig, the ring bearer for the other recent Winter Break wedding we'd attended. She had let out a squeal and run the wrong way. She'd finally been sacked by the groom, but all in all, any attempt at decorum had been destroyed. It was pretty funny, though.

I sighed and stared out the window. The same big, gorgeous white flakes had fallen all during our ceremony. Pastor Taylor had removed the drapes that covered the windows on both sides of the sanctuary. Then he and Odie Rimrucker placed small lights around the outside of the building so that the fat flakes were highlighted as I walked down the aisle. The church was decorated with tiny, sparkling lights and luminous glass snowflakes. And Inez had made the gown of my dreams, just like the one Dela had shown me. And I wore the jewelry she left me. The beautiful green stones helped to draw some of the attention away from my bright red hair. Thanks to Dela, Emily said it definitely didn't look like my head was on fire. I couldn't have asked for more. But the most wonderful part of my wedding was that my father proudly walked me down the aisle, my mother cried, and I married the most handsome, incredible man in the world.

The church had been packed to the rafters. It was as if everyone in Winter Break had turned out. And they just might have. Including Bertha Pennypacker. Of course, it would have been difficult for her to have not been there, seeing that she was one of my bridesmaids. Yes, a bridesmaid. After I nominated her to be the president of the library board, things began to change for us. *Nothing so broken that God can't mend it.* Emily, my matron of honor, and all my other bridesmaids had welcomed her with open arms, helping her to feel as if she fit right in. I couldn't help but glance at her as I approached the front of the church. I'd never seen her look so happy. I was determined she was going to stay that way if I had anything to say about it.

Dewey was Amos's best man. I was thrilled to have my old friend involved in my wedding. I was even happier to finally shake hands with Amos's father. After my insistence, Amos had contacted him. After years of estrangement because of his dad's drinking, I won't say that things weren't a little tense, but it was a work in progress. I was confident that one of these days, they would be able to put the past behind them and develop a real father and son relationship. *Nothing so broken that God can't mend it.*

It had taken a few days to calm my mother down when she found out about Ina Mae's murder and the trap we set for J.D. "You're just like that Jessica Fletcher in *Murder She Wrote*," she'd snapped. "Everyone around her dropped dead. I'm surprised there was anyone left alive. Winter Break is your Cabot Cove." As much as I'd loved *Murder She Wrote*, I'd always had suspicions about Jessica. I mean, how many people have to die before you look at the one person who was always nearby? And she makes her living writing mystery novels? Please. However, I had no intention of debating the point with my mother, especially since I'd been a murder suspect for a little while myself. At least now Mom was enjoying being a mother-in-law. Jessica Fletcher, Cabot Cove, and Winter Break's murder rate were all on a back burner while she began to meddle not only in my life but also in her son-in-law's. Funny thing was, Amos loved it. Since his own mother had passed away a few years earlier, having someone clucking over him and getting into his business made him feel like he had a mom again. I was very grateful for my mother, not only for making my husband happy, but for joining forces with Inez Baumgartner. Together they had created the wedding of my dreams. Of course, I didn't credit them for sending the snow. In my heart, I believed it was a wedding gift from God.

"Sheriff Hitchens gave me your keys after the ceremony," Amos said. "I'm glad the KBI found them in Dela's car where she dropped them, but it would have been nice if they'd told us earlier."

"The important thing is that we got them back. And by the way, they're *our* keys now. In fact, everything is ours. It feels good to share everything with someone you love, doesn't it?" He didn't answer me, but another long kiss told me he felt the same way.

A few weeks earlier, I'd compared a wedding to a funeral, but I'd discovered I was wrong about that.

After attending two funerals, one for Dela and another for Ina Mae, I realized that funerals were a way to say good-bye to a life that was over while weddings were a way to say hello to a life that was beginning. A big difference.

"We're going to have to send thank-you cards for all the gifts," I said, looking over the stack of presents piled up on a table against the wall. Amos and I would never need a toaster again as long as we lived, and we had enough crystal goblets to supply Ruby's café should she ever decide to get really fancy. I got up from my chair and got a large envelope from the top of the stack. "I think you'll be interested in this one. I haven't had time to open it."

"What is it?"

I plopped back down in the chair next to him. "What do you think it is?"

He sat up straight and his eyes got big. "Is it—is it. . ."

I put my fingers on his lips. "Stop before you hurt yourself. Yes, Ruby gave it to me."

"Open it. Open it."

Men and meat. Sheesh. I slowly opened the envelope, just because I knew it would drive him crazy. I pulled out a card congratulating us on our wedding. Tucked inside the card was a folded piece of paper. I unfolded it and started to read.

Dear Ivy and Amos,

I've only given this recipe to one other

person outside my family. That was Bitty Flanagan, your aunt. But now I want to give it to you. I ask you not to pass it along to anyone else until I'm gone and then only to people you can trust. It isn't that it's such a big secret, but as long as everyone thinks it is, it makes it special. Hope you understand.

I could never thank you both enough for bringing my Bert back to me. This isn't even close, but here's the other part of my gift. Free Redbird Burgers for as long as I live—and Bert lives. After that, I can't guarantee anything. Ha ha.

All my love,

Ruby Bird

What followed was the recipe for Redbird Burgers. There weren't really any surprises. I'd already guessed at most of the ingredients.

"Well, what's this secret component everyone's been trying to get their hands on?" Amos asked. "I don't see anything that unusual."

"Wait a minute. There's more." Down at the bottom of the page Ruby's scrawled handwriting began again.

People in Winter Break have been trying to find out my secret ingredient for years. Now I'm going to tell it to you. (over) I flipped the paper over and there it was. *My secret ingredient is prayer. I pray over every single burger. That's my way of knowing that I've lifted almost every person in Winter Break up to God. I ask God's blessings over everyone who eats one of my burgers. I pray that their family would walk in health, peace, and prosperity. And I pray that they all find God's will for their lives. I hope you're not disappointed, but I think taking time to pray for someone else is the greatest "ingredient" there is in this life. Don't you?*

"Well, I'll be switched," Amos said with amazement. "All this time we thought she was putting some top-secret ingredient in her burgers, and she was. Just not the kind we had in mind."

"Oh, Amos," I said, laying my head on his shoulder. "Winter Break is really a special place, isn't it?"

He nodded. "I've always thought so."

I kissed him again. "And you don't mind going on our honeymoon in the spring?"

"No. I'm glad we decided to stay here for the winter." He kissed my earlobe. "The funny thing is, there isn't anywhere else in the world I want to be more than here, in this house, with you. To me, this is the perfect honeymoon."

Mom and Dad were staying in Hugoton for a couple of days so Amos and I could have some time alone. Then they would stay with us for another week before heading back to China. I would miss them, but now I had my own family. I wasn't alone anymore. Pal made a growling noise in his sleep and Miss Skiffins patted his nose to tell him to settle down.

"I've got an idea. . ." I started to say.

"Oh no. Not again," Amos said, smiling.

"No, not that kind of idea." I watched the snow dance in front of us like it was celebrating our wedding. "I've got an idea about Winter Break."

Amos kissed my cheek. "And what is it?"

"Winter Break is not so much a town as it is a place inside the heart. Everyone has a spot where they belong, right in the center of God's will. It's a special place where you find your heart's desires and where miracles happen all the time. But to find it, you have to lay down all your own ideas and plans. You must give God everything you thought you owned. That's when you will find your own Winter Break. It's out there for all of God's children. He's already prepared it." I hugged Amos. "What do you think about that?"

He laughed. "I think you're delirious. Let's go upstairs."

I stood up and checked the lock on the back door. Pal woke up and watched me. He and Miss Skiffins liked to sleep in my bedroom, but I was thinking that tonight they might have to get comfortable in the guest room. I stopped in front of the tapestry and stared at it. Amos came up behind me and put his arms around me.

"It's really special, isn't it?" he said.

"Yes, it is." Aunt Bitty waved to me from the bench by the lake. She watched Amos and me skating together on the frozen lake with a knowing smile on her face. Even though she wasn't with me physically at my wedding, I'd felt her presence the entire time. It was my aunt Bitty who introduced me to Winter

Break when I was a child, and Aunt Bitty who led me back as an adult. Her legacy was one of love, faith, and destiny. I was determined that someday I would give to someone else what she'd given to me. I kissed my fingertips and reached up to press them to her painted face.

And with that, my new husband and I marched upstairs, ready to begin our new life together. Behind us, a small calico cat and a very contented border collie brought up the rear.

Ruby's Redbird Burger

(This recipe makes 4 one-pound burgers or 8 half-pound burgers. Ruby's are actually one-pound monsters, but yours can be smaller!)

Cook 8 slices of peppered bacon in large skillet. Cook until crisp. Remove from skillet and set aside.

Remove all bacon grease from the pan except for approximately 2 tablespoons. (Set aside the remaining grease.) In grease, sauté half a large, chopped white onion, along with 2 tablespoons finely chopped jalapeños. (Canned or from a jar are fine.) Cook until soft.

Season 4 pounds hamburger (80/20) with:
Sautéed onions and jalapeños
4 tablespoons Ruby's Burger Mix (See recipe below.)

Knead seasonings into hamburger, but do not overwork the meat. Make 8 (or 16) patties. You can use a hamburger mold or a large mayonnaise lid to shape the burgers into a consistent size.

Place approximately 1 ounce shredded extra sharp or sharp cheddar cheese in the middle of each patty. Do not go all the way to the edges. Sprinkle approximately

1 tablespoon crumbled peppered bacon on top of the cheese. Then place another patty on top, and crimp the edges to totally seal the burger.

Cook over moderate heat in skillet seasoned with bacon grease. Once both sides are browned, cover skillet to keep burgers juicy. Cook to desired doneness. Do not turn burgers more than twice. Add 2 slices sharp cheddar cheese on top right before you remove the burgers.

Slice remaining half of onion and cook in remaining grease until rings are soft and fairly translucent. Add onions to top of burgers. Place on large deli buns (toast the buns in the oven with real butter). Follow with lettuce, slice of tomato, small spoonful of pickle relish, and mustard. You can make a special mustard using Dijon with a little horseradish or simply use regular yellow mustard. (This is Ruby's choice. She doesn't cotton to that fancy schmancy mustard!) *Do not ever use ketchup on a Ruby's Redbird burger. If Ruby finds out, you will never be allowed to eat another Redbird Burger again!*

Redbird Burger Mix

(This makes more than enough for the recipe)

3 tablespoons kosher salt
4 tablespoons coarse black pepper
2 tablespoons dry minced garlic
½ to 1 tablespoon dry crushed red pepper, to taste
½ tablespoon paprika

Mix all dry ingredients together and store in an airtight container. Does not need to be refrigerated. This mix also works as a steak rub!

Don't forget the most important ingredient for a Ruby's Redbird Burger—prayer! Ruby prays for everyone who orders a burger. She prays that God will bless them with health, prosperity, a heart to hear from God, and the willingness to follow Him wherever He leads. For anyone eating a Redbird Burger, the victim. . .I mean, customer's health could probably use a double dose of prayer!

Nancy Mehl's novels are all set in her home state of Kansas. "Although some people think of Kansas as nothing more than flat land and cattle, we really are quite interesting!" she says.

Nancy is a mystery buff who loves the genre and is excited to see more inspirational mysteries becoming available to readers who share her passion. Her "Ivy Towers Mystery Series" combines two of her favorite things—mystery and snow.

"Unfortunately, our past several winters have been pretty dry. I enjoy writing fiction because I can make it snow as much as I want!"

Nancy works for the City of Wichita, assisting low-income seniors and the disabled. Her volunteer group, Wichita Homebound Outreach, seeks to demonstrate the love of God to special people who need to know that someone cares.

She lives in Wichita, Kansas, with her husband of thirty-five years, Norman. Her son, Danny, is a graphic designer who has designed several of her book covers. They attend Word of Life Church.

Her Web site is www.nancymehl.com.

You may correspond with this author by writing:

Nancy Mehl
Author Relations
PO Box 721
Uhrichsville, OH 44683

A Letter to Our Readers

Dear Reader:
In order to help us satisfy your quest for more great mystery stories, we would appreciate it if you would take a few minutes to respond to the following questions. We welcome your comments and read each form and letter we receive. When completed, please return to:

Fiction Editor
Heartsong Presents—MYSTERIES!
PO Box 721
Uhrichsville, Ohio 44683

Did you enjoy reading *For Whom the Wedding Bell Tolls* by Nancy Mehl?

Very much! I would like to see more books like this! The one thing I particularly enjoyed about this story was:

___

___

___

Moderately. I would have enjoyed it more if:

___

___

___

Are you a member of the HP—MYSTERIES! Book Club?
Yes No

If no, where did you purchase this book?

___

Please rate the following elements using a scale of 1 (poor) to 10 (superior):

___ Main character/sleuth

___ Romance elements

___ Inspirational theme

___ Secondary characters

___ Setting

___ Mystery plot

How would you rate the cover design on a scale of 1 (poor) to 5 (superior)? ___

What themes/settings would you like to see in future **Heartsong Presents—MYSTERIES!** selections? ___

___

___

___

Please check your age range:

- Under 18
- 18–24
- 25–34
- 35–45
- 46–55
- Over 55

Name: ___

Occupation: ___

Address: ___

E-mail address: ___

MYSTERIES!

Heartsong Presents—MYSTERIES! provide romance and faith interwoven among the pages of these fun whodunits. Written by the talented and brightest authors in this genre, such as Christine Lynxwiler, Cecil Murphey, Nancy Mehl, Dana Mentink, Candice Speare, and many others, these cozy tales are sure to challenge your mind, warm your heart, touch your spirit—and put your sleuthing skills to the test.

Not all titles may be available at time of order.
If outside the U.S., please call
740-922-7280 for shipping charges.

SEND TO: **Heartsong Presents—Mysteries** Readers'! Service
P.O. Box 721, Uhrichsville, Ohio 44683
Please send me the items checked above. I am enclosing $_____
(please add $3.00 to cover postage per order. OH add 7% tax. WA add 8.5%). Send check or money order—no cash or C.O.D.s, please.
To place a credit card order, call 1-740-922-7280.

NAME ________________________________

ADDRESS ______________________________

CITY/STATE ____________________ ZIP________